SISTER FUNTIME

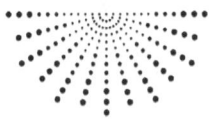

SISTER FUNTIME

A SMILEYLAND STORY

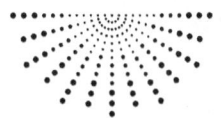

SPENCER HAMILTON

NerdyWordsmith

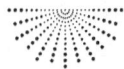

"*A*nyone heard the stories about this place? About *Mister Smiley*?"

The others scoffed at the way Brad said the name—posed like Frankenstein's monster, arms raised, voice dripping with Vincent Price intonations—but Cam felt a shiver skitter along his spinal column as they approached the abandoned amusement park.

"Legend says that on this night, *Halloween*, thirty years ago, a *killer* was born . . ."

It was late, nearly midnight. Cam had a suspicion that Brad had intentionally miscalculated how long the drive would be to reach this place. Anything to heighten the drama—that was Brad. Even now, as they reached the end of the deserted parking lot, Amy's Toyota Corolla parked in a far corner, Brad was hamming it up for them, trying to get a reaction with another one of his bullshit stories. He swung his flashlight's beam upward, slicing through the darkness that seemed to swallow up everything around it, until it came to rest over giant letters towering above them:

WELCOME TO SMILEYLAND!

Cam had never heard of the place, but he'd only moved from across the pond last semester. Despite his secret fear, a part of him listened intently to Brad's story, hungry for more information.

"And he visits SMILEYLAND"—Brad practically shouted the name, making Cam and Jess jump and Amy roll her eyes—"every Hallow's Eve, hungry for more victims . . ."

Amy slapped both hands onto her cheeks in mock fright. "Oh no, Brad—Halloween? That's *tonight*!"

"Shut up, Amy, some of us take this seriously."

Brad went to shove her playfully, but Amy dodged him and skipped through the turnstiles beneath the entrance. Jess followed quickly behind, the yellow daisy in her hair glowing in the darkness like a beacon. Cam adjusted his glasses and craned his neck to see the words painted on the wooden facing beneath the gigantic bulb-filled letters.

WHERE THE ONLY RULE
IS TO NEVER STOP SMILING!

Another shiver shot down his spine.

Brad nudged him. "Back me up here, Cam."

Cam smiled apologetically and followed the girls past the turnstiles, calling over his shoulder, "Leave me out of this."

"Me too," Jess said, hands on hips, staring around at the dark amusement park. "While y'all fight it out, I'm gonna go find somewhere to go to the bathroom."

She trotted off and was soon swallowed by the night.

Cam would have liked for them all to stick together, but he kept quiet, cataloging their surroundings.

They'd entered a large courtyard. Trash rustled lightly along the cobblestones in the late October wind. Opposite the entrance was a large fountain, dried up over the years. Past the fountain was what appeared to be a number of animatronic woodland creatures in various stages of decay. Looming over all of this, like watchful giants, were the silhouettes of a Ferris wheel on the left and a massive rollercoaster on the right, the full moon grinning down between them.

"Anyway . . ." Brad said, standing in the middle of the courtyard with his flashlight angled beneath his chin, casting his features in light and shadow like a jack-o'-lantern, "story goes, little Timmy was the happiest boy alive when his parents brought him to Smileyland. But something was wrong with Timmy. His parents were afraid of him. They kept him locked up, ignoring his pleas to go to Smileyland . . ."

Cam almost jumped at a sound somewhere in the distance. He stared in its direction, willing his eyes to see what was out there, but it was all a void of blackness. He turned back to Brad and joined Amy as a reluctant audience, but he couldn't help but feel as if someone were out there . . . watching.

"Until Halloween, thirty years ago," Brad continued, grinning at each of them in turn. One hand shone the flashlight across his features, the other unconsciously gripping his belt buckle. It was the one he always wore, made to look like a hockey mask. Like those slasher films he was always going on about. "They finally gave him his wish . . ."

Cam glanced around, thinking, *Who would wish to come*

to this place? Even in broad daylight, in its heyday, he couldn't imagine Smileyland ever being anything but creepy.

Brad went on, staring straight at Cam. "But they *left* him here. *Forever.*"

Cam tried to swallow. His throat gave a dry click.

"Nobody knows," Brad said, "what happened to him after the park closed down—"

"AAAAIIIIIIIIII—!"

The scream pierced the night. It held on for an impossibly long time, then ominously cut short, its echo swallowed in the silence that followed.

Cam spun around, staring into the night. "Who's out there?" His voice cracked. His heart sped up. Why'd they only bring the one flashlight? Why'd they come here at all?

Amy didn't seem as impressed. She stalked up to Brad and yanked his hoodie's drawstrings, scowling. "Okay, Brad, very funny. You got Jess in on your little joke . . ." But something in Brad's expression made her trail off. Cam could see the hesitation in her eyes.

Brad shook his head vehemently, his flashlight wheeling around as he attempted to shine it in every dark corner. "No, I didn't plan this, I swear. I don't—"

"Let's put a *smile* on that face . . ."

Jess came leaping out of the darkness, her mane of red hair flowing behind her in the autumn wind.

"BOO!"

Now she was on her knees in the middle of their little group, laughing. Brad and Amy quickly joined in, but Cam could tell he hadn't been the only one she'd managed to scare.

"You should have seen your face!" Jess said, pointing up at Brad. "Gave you a taste of your own medicine!" She clambered back to her feet. "Besides, your story sucks."

Brad looked genuinely hurt. "You didn't even let me finish it!"

Jess shrugged, threading the daisy back into her hair. "You were telling it all wrong. It wasn't thirty years ago, it was twenty. The kid's name wasn't Timmy, it was Johnnie. His parents didn't just leave him here, they up and disappeared. And tonight's called *All* Hallows' Eve. And, finally, don't try denying that you were just gonna give us some bullshit scare at the end like Freddy Krueger was about to pop out and cut one of our heads off."

Brad folded his arms. "Fine, see if you could tell it better, then!"

Jess held out a hand. "Flashlight, please."

Reluctantly, Brad handed it over.

"Everyone knows the story of Mister Smiley. That's boring. So I'm gonna tell y'all a story I bet you never heard before." As she spoke, Jess stepped slowly across the cobblestones toward the path that wound past the Ferris wheel. She grinned back at them. "Follow me if you dare."

Brad, never one to spoil the fun, shrugged and followed along. Amy took Cam by the arm, whispering, "Come on, we gotta stick together!" and giggling. They all strolled along the gently curving path, deeper and deeper into Smileyland.

Jess, in the lead, turned and walked backward, shining the flashlight up into her own face. "I'm gonna tell y'all a story of this place *before* it was Smileyland.

Back when all that stood here was an old orphanage. I'm gonna tell y'all the story . . ."

Again, that feeling of being watched struck Cam. He shivered.

". . . of Sister Funtime."

I

*S*unlight streamed down from the heavens upon Dorothea Annabeth Chesterton as she knocked on the front door, thrilling at God's infinite wisdom in sending her to St. Teresa's Joyous Youths Orphanage.

Inwardly, she scolded herself. Dory Chesterton she was no longer; her new name, taken into eternity upon union with her God, was now Sister Mary Matthew.

She knocked again, straightening her back and imagining herself as this Mary. In truth, she'd struggled with her identity change from the first, and often caught herself thinking as the old Dorothea. Dory was fun, silly even, given to flights of imagination and always letting her mind wander while in school. Sister Mary Matthew, she'd decided, held a bottomless well of resolve which manifested as an almost supernatural patience with children; never would she scold a child for giving in to the temptations of childhood. Yes—the children of St. Teresa's would look upon her, beam unabashedly, and then resume their games, feeling safe and cared for with Sister Mary Matthew until their new parents had found them.

A sudden clap of thunder made her jump, clutching a hand to the crucifix resting upon her habit and emitting a quiet squeak of surprise. She turned to find that the sunshine was now hidden behind a dour bank of clouds, and she watched them excitedly, waiting to see a fork of lightning. None came. She chided herself again—she'd let the weather take her by surprise and had fallen into her old habits, her *Dory* habits, getting lost in her imagination.

The door jostled in its frame and creaked open, and she turned to it again as Sister Mary Matthew.

"Oh!" she exclaimed, unable to hide her smile.

Standing at the threshold was a child. A stout, chubby little thing, a boy of perhaps three or four, his chin shiny with drool. He stared up at her, unguarded.

"Why, hello," she said, bending down to greet him at eye level. "And who might you be? The master of this household?"

He giggled. Before he could answer, however, a stern voice threw itself from the darkness behind him.

"Mister—Thomas!"

For a brief moment, the sister witnessed a look of terror flit across the child's cherubic expression, and his little shoulders tensing up, before the owner of that voice stepped from the shadows.

"Sneaking off again, young man? Back to your cot immediately with you. And for the love of St. Teresa, wipe your nose!"

The boy trundled up a long staircase, one hand clinging to the rail above his head. Sister Mary settled her attention upon the woman who had taken his place: a nun in full dress, her expression as stern as her voice, her skin creased not by age but by perpetually glowering at God's children in disapproval.

She leveled this gaze upon Sister Mary and said, "Well. You must be the new sister. Follow me, then."

Sister Mary stepped across the threshold, leaving the darkening weather behind for the sultry, airless atmosphere inside. St. Teresa's was a largish two-story mansion that appeared to wallow in its neglect. Cobwebs draped the shadows, and already she felt dust mites tickling her nose. The wallpaper seemed days away from curling off the walls, and the sickly yellow light from the chandelier spread only so far before being swallowed in the house's gothic aspirations.

This surly, unnamed sister led her to the left of the staircase, through an open living area, to a corner office, tidier yet somehow even frowzier, whose furniture dwarfed the small space. The sister sat herself behind a sturdy oak desk and nodded to the armchair opposite her. Mary sat, a puff of dust almost causing her to sneeze; she felt like a child herself in such a large armchair, almost comical in its size, as if she'd snuck into the realm of the giants at the end of Jack's beanstalk.

"Welcome to St. Teresa's Joyous Youths Orphanage, Sister . . ." The older woman consulted an open filing folder of papers on the desk before her, which was similarly covered in neat stacks of paper. ". . . Mary Matthew, so it is. I am Sister Agatha Eustace, and I run this orphanage. You will answer to me during your stay, but there may come the time when our benefactor, the Good Samaritan who owns this building and funds our work, may visit."

Mary sat forward so that she could be in clear view of the sister. A gorgeous, intricately painted ceramic figurine of the Virgin Mary stood at the desk's head, directly between them, smiling serenely at Mary. She nodded at the older sister, trying on her most radiant smile. "Yes. Thank you so very much, Sister Eustace, God bless you. I feel so loved to be given this chance to serve our Lord's most innocent."

The sister stared at her, her expression hard but blank. "Yes, well. As I've said, you'll answer to me while you are under this roof. You will find that I run a tight ship."

The unspoken implication of her words, it seemed to Mary, was *I run this house, not God,* and it was so bold a sentiment that Mary felt in scandalous awe of this older woman.

"There are twenty-three children currently staying here. Eleven boys and twelve girls. The youngest is merely a baby and the oldest has just turned seventeen. Twenty-three may seem like a small number to you, but I assure you, Sister, it is enough to keep your hands full and then some."

Mary nodded, absorbing every word. "I love children," she broke in, beaming.

Again, that hard, blank stare, as if Sister Eustace didn't believe such a statement could possibly be true.

"Um," Mary said, itching under that stare. "How long has this orphanage served the children, Sister?"

Sister Eustace blinked, as if baffled as to why anyone would wonder such a thing. "Mr. James—the benefactor I mentioned—bought and renovated this building and its surrounding environs some fifty odd years ago, 1868 or perhaps '69. I am unaware of its purpose before that, but he claims it is quite old, even for these parts. To be frank, Sister Mary, this building's history does not concern you.

Today is all that matters. I'd advise you to turn your will to the work at hand."

Mary nodded, inclining her head and attempting to hide the heat that flooded her cheeks at the chastisement. "Of course," she murmured.

"Our days start with morning prayer at six thirty sharp," Sister Eustace went on brusquely. "You shall be in charge of the under-fives. You saw the schoolhouse and chapel on either side of us as you entered the property"—she gestured to her left and right, though neither building could be seen through the office window at her back, which had its curtains tightly drawn—"and farther back you will also find a greenhouse and cemetery. Under no circumstance should you enter the basement." She gave no explanation for this last remark, but she waited for a response from Mary, who nodded. "The children's sleeping quarters are upstairs, boys' ward to the right and girls' ward to the left. Your own sleeping quarters are on this floor. Sister Ines Joseph!"

This last came as a barked command, so loud as to almost make Mary jump in her seat. A figure promptly appeared in the doorway.

"Sister?"

"Please take our new arrival, Sister Mary Matthew" —she nodded across the desk to Mary in her armchair— "and show her to her room."

"Yes, Sister," the woman at the door said.

And just like that, Mary saw, she was no longer welcome in Sister Eustace's office. The older sister had already turned her attention to the myriad papers stacked upon her desk, not even sparing a goodbye nod.

The instant she'd stepped from the office, side by side with Sister Ines, Mary found the weight of first impressions lifted from her shoulders. That weight didn't return with this new sister, for Mary could tell that she was the antithesis of Sister Eustace. Whereas the head sister filled her with intimidation, she found herself instantly drawn to Sister Ines, like a magnet. The woman was quite large in stature, and yet her movements were fluid and graceful. Her skin was a creamy brown and beautiful. Mary couldn't even begin to guess at the woman's age—thirty? fifty?

"Welcome to hell, Sister," were Ines's first words to her. Mary almost stopped dead in her tracks from the shock of such a thing being uttered about such a place. Ines saw the surprise in Mary's face and laughed, a soft giggle like sleigh bells. "Merely a joke. You do know of jokes, yes? You'll need a sense of humor to survive this place. Without mine, I'd have wrung Eustace's wrinkled old neck by now."

Mary gave a nervous laugh as they passed through the kitchen. "The sister did seem . . . intense."

Ines nodded. "Sister Killjoy, that's what some of the children call her."

Mary covered her mouth to stifle a much louder, surprised laugh.

Through the kitchen and down a hallway, Ines paused at an open doorway and grinned at her. "Killjoy . . . perfect name for her, no? Children have a gift when it comes to seeing the truth behind the veil."

She ushered Mary into a small, modest room, completely bare besides a small cot, a dresser, and a beautiful mahogany miniature cross hanging on the wall opposite the bed. There was a small window on the far wall, but thick black curtains shrouded it, not allowing a single strand of sunlight inside.

"Speaking of Killjoy," Ines said, nodding to the window, "she is convinced that too much sunshine leads to sin. We are required to leave the curtains drawn at all times. I'm honestly surprised she hasn't had them boarded up."

"This is my room?" Mary asked.

Ines nodded, then inclined her head further down the hall. "I'm only separated from you by a single wall, so I'll hear everything you do and say. Beware." She whispered the last word, a twinkle in her eye, and Mary smiled in reply. "It's not much," Ines continued, "but you'll be spending most of your time elsewhere. The sister has made it abundantly clear that our personal living quarters are strictly meant for personal prayer, and maybe sleep if it can't be helped."

Mary approached the bed, fully aware that Ines was still watching her. Had the sister noticed the lack of a suitcase in her hands? Sister Eustace hadn't commented on the fact, had perhaps not noticed or cared, but now . . .

She knelt, blocking Ines's view with her shoulder as she surreptitiously snaked one hand beneath her habit and collected everything she owned in the world: a small bundle wrapped in a ratty nightgown. She unwrapped the rosary beads and pocket Bible, printed on onion paper, and tucked them beneath the thin pillow and stood.

Ines didn't comment on what she saw, for which Mary was immensely grateful. Together they toured the rest of the property, and Mary's excitement grew in full earnest this time, without the presence of Sister Eustace to temper it. The gravel driveway circled a stone fountain at the entrance to the property (where the taxicab had deposited Mary when she first arrived), most of which was gently shaded by surrounding pines. On one side of the mansion sat a single-room schoolhouse and on the other a neat little whitewashed chapel, its steeple topped with a plain white cross. A path wound between them and behind the mansion, where Mary found the greenhouse. Beyond that was hidden an overgrown and gated cemetery. When Ines took her back to the mansion, to the back door leading into the kitchen, Mary stopped and turned to look across the property.

"Wow," she breathed.

Ines looked with her. "Yes. Quite beautiful."

The orphanage stood on the smallest of hills, with the grassy expanse gently sloping down toward the greenhouse and cemetery. This afforded them the view of a veritable ocean of pines sweeping outward and all around for what seemed like miles. The orphanage was an oasis in an endless forest. Mary was certain she'd never lain eyes on such natural beauty.

Ines nudged her. "Come," she said, taking Mary's hand and sending a confused jumble of butterflies through her stomach. "Time to meet the children!"

$\mathcal{M}$ary's first week at St. Teresa's was both the most difficult and happiest of her life.

To be a nun at the Joyous Youths Orphanage was to experience constant whiplash between the two. Happiness when she was with her charges, the sweet children of St. Teresa's; difficulty when dealing with St. Teresa's tyrannical ruler, Sister Agatha Eustace.

Or, to call her by her other name . . . Sister Killjoy.

Secretly, Mary had taken to using that nickname almost from the first. Only ever privately (even once in her personal prayers, the name had slipped into her thoughts and she'd instantly wanted to commit self-flagellation for the sin), and certainly never to the children, though she'd once heard Lizzie whisper *"something-something* Sister Killjoy!" to Benjamin during breakfast. Mary refused to encourage such behavior, though privately she agreed with Ines that children had a knack for seeing behind the masks adults often wore.

Of the seven children Mary was in charge of—the "under-fives," as Eustace had referred to the youngest of the orphans—her favorites were the twins, little Haley and Hanna. Proving to have matching mischievous streaks as wide as their smiles, the twins were always showing up where they weren't supposed to be. And yet, Mary could not help falling madly in love with them at every turn. They were gentle yet charming, and the way they cheered each other on with boundless encourage-ment made Mary's heart ache with longing to experience such connection, such unassumingly devout companion-ship. That would not happen—not in this life, not after her commitment to her omnipotent Heavenly Father—and so she instead lived vicariously through these four-year-old angels with white-blond hair and matching ice-blue eyes.

Perhaps it was this longing for companionship which drew her to Ines. It was hard to say, for her thoughts and her heart were pulled in a million directions ever since she'd arrived at the orphanage. One thing was unavoid-ably true: Mary had never felt so strong a compulsion, again making her think of opposite poles of a magnet finally coming face to face, as she felt now toward Sister Ines Joseph. Her infatuation with the sister was secretly frightening, secretly invigorating.

She remembered the first secret Ines shared with her —after the "Sister Killjoy" secret, of course. It had been later that very night. Mary had spent several fruitless hours on her bruised knees praying for comfort yet feeling nothing. Where she ached for a response from her Lord there was only the lonely void of her own heart staring back at her. She was lying on her cot trying to not make a sound with her weeping. Ines had burst into her room—the sisters' doors must never be closed, according to the strict Sister Eustace—and pulled her through the dark, ominous house to the kitchen back door and along the footpath toward the cemetery. Hidden in the overgrowth behind the last grave markings was, of all things, a rusty bicycle.

"My only worldly possession," Ines confided, smiling conspiratorially in the moonlight. "No taxicab would drive a brown woman this far upstate, so I rode my bicycle. I had an inkling I might be made to forfeit it upon arrival, so I stored it here before making my presence known."

"But," Mary whispered, her mind reeling, nearly drunk with the giddy feel of a shared secret, "whatever could you keep it for?"

"Small rebellions are good for the heart, Sister," were Ines's only words.

Later that week, Mary convinced Ines to let her use one of the rubber wheels of the bicycle for a game of hoop rolling with the children. A few of the older children even joined in the fun, and at one point—Mary smiled at this memory—she scooped up the tire in a moment of inspiration and threaded herself through the middle, so that she held it in a circle around her waist. All the children stopped, waiting to see what the new nun was up to. She spun the tire clockwise, rolling her hips to catch the rubber so that it continued rolling around and around, her arms held up for balance. The children shrieked and laughed and clapped and Mary was reminded once again why she had taken up this vocation in the first place.

Later that same day, during her children's naptime, she'd gone out to return the tire only to discover it missing. Also missing was the small, thin pillow from her cot, and the rosary beads she had tucked beneath it.

"Sister Eustace is God at St. Teresa's," Ines told her. "Old Testament."

Mary frowned at this. Confiscating personal amenities like pillows and prayer beads wasn't an Old Testament wrath-of-a-jealous-God punishment. It was the act of a petulant child lashing out for not getting her way.

But Sister Ines's words were illustrated most clearly partway through Mary's second week. It was afternoon naptime for her charges, during which time Mary would often stand and smile with all of her heart at the delicate little features of the slumbering children. On this day, however, Mary was feeling restless, unbalanced, and so she stole from the nursery, slipped outside, and darted into the modest chapel for a quick check-in with God.

Sitting among the pews, her shimmering vision settled on Jesus on his cross, she poured her love for her Savior outward with all of her heart. Once again, she got no response that she could discern. Still, she prayed.

When a voice *did* come, it was not speaking to her. She strained her ears and just made out a whisper coming from the crucified Jesus statue.

"I just *know* the old bitch keeps it here somewhere!"

Mary nearly gasped at the words. At the language. Had she . . . imagined it?

"Bet she drinks it herself. Otherwise the cunt would dry out to nothing but dust!"

Mary clamped a hand over her gaping mouth.

Hesitantly, slowly, she crept past the pews toward Jesus. The whispers—a boy and a girl—hadn't come from the statue but from behind it. Muffled clattering, giggles, a glugging noise, and something quieter, indiscernible. A small door led her into the chapel's back room, a cramped vestry even smaller than her own private quarters. Inside she found—

"Lizzie?" she asked. "Benjamin!"

Ines's two oldest charges, the girl seventeen and the boy fourteen, were huddled inside, pawing at each other and kissing messily. If she hadn't known only minutes had passed, she would have thought they were drunk. A communion bottle swung from Lizzie's grip, its frothy red contents already nearing empty.

"Oh, shit!" Lizzie said, then doubled over in laughter.

Benjamin had the sense to act guilty. His cheeks flushed with embarrassment and he stumbled away from the older girl, trying to discreetly hold his hands in front of his crotch.

The truth of the matter came to Mary at once. These children had snuck away to drink communion wine and engage in lustful, carnal acts under the Lord's roof. If Eustace were to discover them, Ines would be the one to face her Old Testament wrath. *An eye for an eye.*

A still, small voice whispered to her: *Small rebellions are good for the heart, Sister.*

Mary straightened. Like a bolt of lightning, she knew what she must do.

"S-Sister," Benjamin stuttered, "we're sorry, it was an accident—"

Mary closed the vestry door behind her, cutting off his words.

"Save your excuses," she said. "I don't need God's all-knowing wisdom to see what's going on."

Lizzie straightened, solemn-faced. Perhaps the weight of impending consequences had caught up with her too. She hastily placed the open communion bottle on the shelf built into the wall and stepped away from it, as if she'd never touched it.

The end of naptime loomed, and Mary had to act fast. Her charges, thankfully, took to their naps like stones, but what would Eustace say if she happened upon seven unattended children?

Quickly, all the while painfully aware of the Jesus statue just on the other side of this thin wall and of the crucifix dangling from her neck, she told the two teenagers what would happen next. Realizing they might get out of this without a paddling from Sister Killjoy, they grinned at each other and at Mary.

Before she could hurry away, they turned to her, halfway past the threshold of the back door. "Sister," Lizzie whispered. She noted that the children were holding hands.

"Quickly now," Mary told them, a twinkle in her eye.

"The little ones were right about you," Lizzie called after her. "Their silly little nickname for you."

Mary stopped short halfway across the chapel's aisle. She turned, empty pews on either side. A nickname? For her? She couldn't comprehend such a possibility. After only ten or so days . . . her? After all, Sister Ines didn't have a nickname with the children as far as she knew. A nickname for her, for Mary . . . but did she *want* to know? What if it were mean, something cruel yet girded in truth like "Killjoy"?

Lizzie's voice floated out of the vestry:

"Sister Funtime!"

And then she and Benjamin were gone, scurrying across the grounds back to wherever Ines held their peers.

Sister Funtime . . .

The words chased her as she ran back to the house. Ran? *Flew.*

She felt buoyed up, felt a happiness rarely gleaned in her solitude. The children had a nickname for her. And not a nickname whispered behind her back out of mockery or mutiny, but surely one of respect and possibly love.

Such was her happiness, a giddy rush of spiritual inebriation, that she never once questioned her decision to help Lizzie and Benjamin as she cracked open the door to the basement and tiptoed down the creaky wood planks to a musty, dirt-packed floor. Quickly, she rummaged around the stacked boxes by the grimy light from the narrow, uncurtained window. Surely this place would be the most sensible spot to store excess communion wine—surely, in fact, that would be the very reason Eustace forbade anyone but herself from entering the basement.

Finding nothing in the first stack of boxes, she hurriedly shoved it aside for the one behind. But at her slightest touch, this second stack of boxes, leaning against the stained cement wall, crumbled and disintegrated to the dirt. Whatever these boxes had held was in pieces now too. Maybe papers? She'd seen other boxes full of files and newspapers and forms; perhaps a pipe had leaked directly onto this one over the years and it had been on the verge of annihilation.

One item remained intact, and it lay at her feet among the soggy remnants.

Her eyes widened in delight. It was a smallish but beautiful, ornately carved crucifix. It seemed to shine up at her in the gloom, and there appeared to be sapphires set into Jesus's eyes and tiny, wine-red rubies inlaid as stigmata.

It . . . *sang* to her.

"Mommy?"

A child's distant voice came from above, almost drowned out by some rumbling boiler somewhere behind her, and she snapped out of her trance. The children must be stirring from their naps. She had run out of time.

But as she turned to go, her knee knocked a wooden crate and she heard sloshing. She'd found it! Frantic, she rescued a bottle from the crate, tucked it beneath her habit, and stumbled up the steps.

It was a close call, but Mary managed to subdue the just-waking children long enough so that she could return to the chapel vestry and refill the communion bottle without alerting Sister Eustace. She would have to confide in Ines later about today's turn of events—Ines needed to know, after all, that two of her charges may require a more watchful eye—but Mary was confident that disaster had been averted.

That is, until she returned to her room that very evening.

Mary never learned how Sister Agatha Eustace had found her out, but nevertheless, the older sister was waiting for her, standing beside the dresser so that Mary only spotted her once she'd stepped inside the room.

"Sister—" she said, surprised.

Without a word, Sister Eustace stepped forward and slapped Mary hard across the face. Blood trickled from her nose, staining her only habit. Her cheek burned as if a white-hot brand still pressed against the skin.

Old Testament indeed. Was this an eye for an eye?

Her expression unreadable, Eustace held out one hand, palm up.

"Your necklace, Sister."

"I . . . Sister, I'm sorry, I — "

"Your *necklace*."

Tears sprang to her eyes as she pulled the crucifix chain over her head with shaking hands. Eustace's gnarled fingers clawed over Jesus's vulnerable body.

"Children are to be kept under strict scrutiny at all times. You're lucky they didn't burn the whole house down in your absence." The sister's voice was perfectly calm, but her eyes caught like steel wool. "One more forbidden crusade down into the basement, Sister Mary Matthew, and I will see you out of a home and stripped of your habit forever."

And she whisked out of the room, leaving Mary to her tears. The ringing silence seemed to emanate from the throbbing handprint on her cheek.

That night, Mary curled into the far corner of her cot, refusing to acknowledge Ines when she came to console. She just lay there, shivering, repeating Lizzie's words in her head again and again until sleep took mercy on her.

Sister Funtime . . . Sister Funtime . . . Sister Funtime . . .

III.

*D*espite her overactive imagination and propensity for daydreaming, Mary—young Dory Chesterton back then—never was one to have actual dreams while she slept. Or if she was, she could never remember them once awake. Sister Mary Matthew, on the other hand, dreamt so often and so vividly that she found herself dreading the arrival of night. The first of her dreams came the night after Sister Eustace slapped her for going into the basement.

In her dream, that stained spot on the basement wall bloomed like a wound, and grew and grew until it had discolored the entire house, the entire St. Teresa's property, and a sweeping swath of pine trees encircling it. The soiled patch of land grew darker and darker with stain until, all at once, it crumbled and disintegrated into the earth. When the dust had settled, there was a deep rumbling—or was it music?—for what felt like a hundred years before, thrusting up out of the earth, climbing toward the sky like some nightmarish amusement ride, was a gigantic crucifix.

As it rose, Jesus squirmed on the cross. His eyes were huge, infinitely faceted sapphires, his teeth jagged diamonds. His wounds wept glinting rubies that gushed from him and rained down upon the earth with a chorus of overlapping heartbeats.

He squirmed. He writhed. He wept.

His movements grew more and more agitated until, with a great ripping sound, his body tore itself down the middle . . . and then it was not one man but two children on the cross—Lizzie and Benjamin, lewdly pressing their bodies against each other, tongues slobbering noisily. A flash of lightning saturated the scene in blinding white, and then it wasn't Lizzie and Benjamin on the cross, but Sister Ines and Mary herself.

As Mary kissed her, Ines screamed and crumbled away like wet sand.

Now Mary was falling from the cross, falling, reaching out for his saving hand but finding nothing, nothing. She fell and fell and came crashing down into a lake of frothing, ruby-red communion wine.

She drowned in his blood.

IV.

*W*aking, Mary pressed her face into the cot and choked down her screams.

A week had passed since that first dream—or maybe it was two weeks—yet she'd suffered these terrible visions every single night since. Time had become elusive, illusory.

However many days it was, they had been the worst of her life—things at St. Teresa's had become more difficult than her first week could have prepared her for, and all the joy of serving God's children had dried up like a lake in a desert. Every morning, Ines flowed into her room and gently woke her; the sister was graciously letting Mary sleep through her morning prayers. In truth, Mary hadn't tried speaking to God since Sister Agatha Eustace had slapped her. She couldn't face another refusal to answer her desperate pleas—not from her Heavenly Father, not from the entity to whom she'd devoted her entire life.

But during last night's dream, she'd had an epiphany. A revelation!

In the course of the usual nightmarish imagery, some of Jesus's ruby blood had spilled down and across Mary's habit, which, in typical dream logic, was entirely pure white instead of the black cloth of the real habit, and so it absorbed his blood as if thirsty for it. Immediately, she'd stumbled back and set to scrubbing the bloody stains from her garments—after all, this was her only habit, and what would Eustace say if she came to dinner the next day in such disrepair?

Almost as immediate was the overwhelming sense of shame that washed through her at the thought. This was *his* blood! He, the man who died for her and Ines and the children and, yes, even Eustace. Who was she to scrub it away? Shouldn't she wear his blood with pride, with humility? His word was law, not Eustace's. That old woman may *say* that she was God at St. Teresa's, but that of course was not true.

Now, awake, Mary rolled from the cot to her knees, hard on the floor, her hands clasped tightly to her breast. She closed her eyes and craned her head to the heavens.

"I know what it is you would have me do, Father," she whispered.

As predicted, there was no answer from above. But still, for the first time in what felt like a lifetime, Mary was resolute in what she must do. It was still the early hours of the morning, but she couldn't waste a second more. When Ines came to wake her, she'd find an empty cot.

Without further ado, Mary got to it. What was that saying? *Idle hands are the devil's plaything*? Well, Mary would exorcise the devil with a little elbow grease, and when she was done, clean sunshine would stream in and chase away any and every hint of the devil's presence.

No more would she mope around in this depressive episode; no more would Ines have to take up her slack lest Eustace see Mary neglecting her duties. And if Sister Agatha Eustace saw fit to punish her again? Fine—but it would be done in broad daylight. Not another day would pass in St. Teresa's Joyous Youths Orphanage in dusty shadows and choking mold and neglectful filth. If Mary was to live every day under the threat of being thrown out and stripped of her habit, if she was to be banished back to the life of silly Dory Chesterton, then so be it— but before that happened, she'd do her damnedest to make her mark on this place.

Not that Eustace would catch Mary saying "damnedest" aloud. Mary wouldn't give her that satisfaction.

Pushing up her sleeves and tying the skirt of her habit above her knees, she went to work. She found a bucket and a rag under the kitchen sink, filling one with soapy water and using the other to dust. Sponges she found as well—even a Brillo pad—which she used with the bucketful of sudsy water to scrub the creaky wooden floorboards. It seemed every surface of this place was buried in a thick coating of dust, and by the end of it her eyes were red and streaming, but she was afraid giving in to the sneezes would wake the household and alert them to what she was up to.

Just as the sun threaded its fingers of light over the tips of the pines, Mary brought the couch and armchair cushions and two rugs out back and beat them to within an inch of their life. Their expelled dust hung in the air like pea soup smog from the Big Apple, and the sun shone through the scrim of dust in an eerie blood-red wash.

When Fran, the old lady who cooked the meals and kept up the greenhouse, arrived, she showed the sister where some of the cleaning chemicals were kept — bleach, vinegar, lye — and Mary attacked the inside of the mansion with renewed vigor. The baseboards, lighting fixtures, bannister, fireplace mantel, et cetera. It was sweaty, backbreaking work, but for Mary it was mercifully cathartic. Her hands slowly became red and raw and wrinkled from the chemicals. It felt as if she were scouring her own soul, peeling away the grit and the grime that had accumulated in the last week or so. As the Good Book said: a new heart, a new spirit.

Mary stood, surveying her handiwork, and whispered to herself, "Forgetting what is behind and straining toward what is ahead, I press on."

She wasn't just leaving Dorothea Annabeth Chesterton behind. She was leaving the last week or so behind. Sister Mary Matthew held a bottomless well of resolve — hadn't that been what she'd decided? This habit represented more than her covenant with her Lord; it represented a new life, a fresh start, a new *her*. She couldn't just crumble at the first tribulation placed in her path, even one as formidable as Sister Agatha Eustace. No, she would show that wrinkly old tyrant that Sister Mary Matthew was made of tougher stuff. Sister Mary Matthew was made of bleach and vinegar and lye — she cut through stains to the shiny heart.

A whimper found her ears from above, and then: "Mommy . . . ?"

Slowly, almost drunkenly, trundling down the staircase came none other than little Thomas. Mary smiled. He was the first of the children she'd met at St. Teresa's, and, true to form, he was always wandering away from the other children. She'd noticed he didn't seem to get along with the others, didn't seem to glom on to his peers during playtime in that way that children have, yet she held a soft spot for the boy and for his chubby little smile.

"Good morning, Thomas," she said, keeping her voice low in case the other children still slept. "Did someone forget his morning prayers?"

The three-year-old stood on the bottom step, rubbing his eyes with his little sausage fingers. When he was a bit more awake, he stared through the bannister at the main living area in dumbstruck awe.

Mary giggled, imitating Ines's sleigh-bell laugh as best she could.

"Behold," she said, spreading her arms wide, "I am making all things new!"

Little Thomas didn't respond to this either, still waking up and still staring around at everything Mary had accomplished. Seeing the place through his eyes now, Mary was almost shocked at how much she'd done in just a couple hours. The staircase, foyer, and living area now looked as if she'd somehow transported them in time back to when they were first constructed, the paint still wet; or perhaps as if God had planted a completely different home's living space in this one's stead. Every surface shone as if touched by the light of the heavens, as if Mary had found a way to scrub clean the very air.

Creaking stairs announced the arrival of more children. First came Tabitha, a gangly Black girl who was technically too old to be in the under-fives, but who was almost supernaturally good with the baby. She would have made Ines's charges a whopping seventeen, and so was staying behind for now. She didn't say much, but her eyes shone bright with intelligence. Mary had noticed a haunted expression that often sank itself into her beautiful little features, but she seemed to find solace in the baby. Sure enough, swaddled in her arms was little six-month-old Luke, cooing softly, one chubby hand poking out and resting on Tabitha's cheek.

Next came the two terrors, two-year-old Sean and eighteen-month-old Bevvy. Mary held the secret belief that Sean would grow up to be a bit of a bully, yet the other children seemed to love him. He came frightfully close to bowling into Tabitha as he bulldozed down the stairs, but redheaded and freckled little Bevvy chose that exact moment to reach out and worm her fingers into a hole in his flannel pajamas and tickle him. He squirmed, giggling, and a crisis was averted.

The last to join the others at the bottom of the stairs were the twins, Haley and Hanna. Mary suspected that this was because, unlike the other children, the twins did not let mysterious sounds distract them from their morning prayers. They viewed God through the same lens that most children saw Saint Nicholas, the rosy-cheeked fat man who brought children presents around the world every Christmas Eve. Come rain or shine, nothing stopped them from getting in a word with God about a new puppy or, perhaps, if he didn't mind, dessert for dinner.

It was Hanna who first spoke. She pushed her way to the front of the group of children and stared on her tippytoes over the bannister.

"It's *beautiful*, sister!" she pronounced.

Haley peeked up beside her and her face burst into a perfect replica of Hanna's own amazement.

"Beautiful!"

Both twins held it out as *beauuuuuutiful!*, and Mary almost laughed at herself when she realized her mistake: she'd thought Hanna was speaking to *her*, to Sister Mary Matthew, but she was speaking to her own flesh-and-blood sister.

"Did you do all this by yourself, Sister Mary Matthew?" asked Tabitha, still cradling Luke in her wiry arms.

"It smells yummy!" exclaimed Sean.

Thomas took up a chant: "Sister Funtime! Sister Funtime! Sister Funtime!" He eagerly looked to the others, who giggled but didn't immediately join in. Finally, Sean chimed in, and the others quickly followed suit.

"Sister Funtime! Sister Funtime! Sister Funtime!"

Hearing her nickname filled her with joy, but the increasing volume of the children's voices alarmed her. She looked toward Eustace's office, but the door remained closed. In truth, she wasn't sure where the older nun slept at night, though hopefully, wherever it was, the clatter of breakfast prep from the kitchen was enough to cover the young ones' chanting.

"Children," Mary said, still whispering herself, as she stepped closer to the stairs. "I understand your eagerness to see what all the commotion was, and I'm so sorry to have woken you like this, but am I right in guessing that some of you still owe morning prayers?"

There was an awkward, guilty-sounding silence during which the children glanced among themselves as if hoping someone else would speak up and take the blame.

"It wasn't you that woke them up, Sister."

Mary looked up to see one of Ines's charges

standing at the top of the stairs. Seventeen-year-old Lizzie. Blushing, Mary averted her eyes from the amount of skin showing beneath the girl's too-small nightshirt. She hadn't had any meaningful interactions with the girl since the communion wine incident, though she had woken to find a piece of ribbon candy in a napkin tucked just inside her room and had guessed that it was a thank-you gift for covering for her and Benjamin. She'd scarfed down the candy in a rush, as if frightened God would see her enjoying herself and mistake it for a sin. Or, in his absence, certainly Sister Killjoy.

She blinked up at the girl, confused. "It wasn't?"

Lizzie nodded down at the children. "It was the crying baby."

Mary looked to Luke, frowning. He seemed perfectly quiet as usual when with Tabitha. But judging from her furrowed brow, the girl didn't think all was well. She stepped off the final stair and came hesitantly to Mary, offering her a closer look at the baby boy.

Mary gasped.

"I didn't know what else to do," Tabitha said, tears forming in her eyes. "Lizzie and I held him in turns all night, but he kept whimpering and he feels hot as a coal."

Peeking out of the blanket he was swaddled in, little Luke's pale features were puckered and his eyes were pained. His already thick head of hair, unruly black curls, was slicked across his scalp, and beneath that . . .

Luke had grown a third eye.

Sprouting from his forehead smack dab in the middle, between and above his perfect eyebrows, was a growth of some kind. Mary would have called it a mosquito bite, or perhaps even a cyst, if it were not for the red band of rash perfectly encircling it, like a bull's-eye.

"Oh, Tabitha, you were so sweet to look after him, but you should have come to me," Mary said, pushing her revulsion at what she saw on Luke's forehead back down her throat. Carefully, she took the baby from a reluctant Tabitha, who hovered around Mary still with that expression of anxiety. "This boy needs a doctor!"

Lizzie, still at the top of the staircase, snorted. "Good luck getting Killjoy to agree," she said, and disappeared back into the girls' ward.

Mary froze at this pronouncement. But Ines, who had appeared on the other side of the stairs, stepped forward decisively.

"Upstairs and back to your beds," the other sister announced. "We'll let you know when breakfast is ready. Quickly now, up, up, up!"

She shooed the children, who all obediently climbed back up, including the anxious Tabitha. Then she came and inspected Luke, still cradled in Mary's arms.

"Lizzie is right," Ines sighed. "Eustace will just tell us to pray for him to recover swiftly and be done with it." She made to take the baby from Mary, who pulled away.

"Ines . . ." How could she say such a thing? Could she not tell that this child needed medical care and fast? Even through the blanket, Mary could feel him burning up with fever. "Don't be absurd. We must try!"

Ines did not reply, though her eyes told Mary everything she needed to know.

Sudden tears stung her eyes. "I'd thought better of you, Sister," Mary whispered.

And she turned and strode through the bright, clean living room toward the dark of Eustace's office.

V.

"You are a foolish, stupid girl," Sister Agatha Eustace said.

Just a few weeks under this cruel woman was enough, however, so that her words almost pinged off of the lid that covered Mary's bottomless well of resolve. She took a deep breath and held it until she was confident the tears wouldn't come. She cradled the feverish child and reminded herself why she was here.

"That may be so," she said, speaking with brash confidence to hide the quaver in her voice, "but I am here to protect the children. As are you."

"As—is—the *Lord*!"

Mary paused, taken aback. In all the bullying and hideousness she'd collected from Eustace, never had the older woman voiced a rebuke in anything other than steady, self-righteous tones. She delivered her condemnations of Mary's character in such calm, matter-of-fact speech that it had the effect of making Mary wonder if it was true—if she were in fact as childish or careless or sinful or willfully ignorant as

37

Eustace said. All for little things like her trip to the basement or finding games for the children or a four-year-old not having their Ten Commandments memorized.

But here . . . here Eustace had finally found something to yell about, and it was, of all things, because a sick child needed special care. All the helpless anger Mary had felt toward this woman after losing her crucifix to her came rushing back, a prickly heat on her skin that rivaled Luke's fever.

"Your purpose here, Sister," Eustace continued, "is not to *protect* the children. Protect them?" She gazed around the office, her eyes wide with mockery, as if expecting to find the devil behind the curtains. "Protect them from whom? From what? Miles of forest in every direction, and everything they could possibly need right here at St. Teresa's. Their meals, lessons, and a bed to sleep on, all provided out of the goodness of our Mr. James's heart. I'm sorry to burst whatever savior-fantasy bubble has expanded in your brain, but their *protection* is none of your concern. Your purpose here, Sister, and that of Sister Ines Joseph and even that of myself, is to set these children on the path of righteousness. When a child leaves St. Teresa's Joyous Youths Orphanage and enters the sinful world awaiting them, they must be equipped with their Lord's armor and his shield and his sword. For it is *he* who protects the children, not some silly idiot girl from Syracuse!"

As if to punctuate Eustace's speech, Luke burst into a fretful squall.

"I . . ." Mary swallowed. She was not sure when they started, but tears now wet her cheeks. "I am just as grateful to our benefactor as you are, Sister . . . but the children do *not* have everything they could possibly need here at the orphanage."

As she spoke, again came that surge of anger; Mary felt almost dizzy with it, would not be surprised if her tears evaporated from its heat.

She charged onward: "Luke is a perfect example. Clearly he is severely ill, and neither you or I or any of St. Teresa's work staff, small as it is, can give him the proper care he needs to survive."

A wicked, triumphant grin set itself into Eustace's features—an expression Mary had so far only seen in her nightly dreams—and she leaned forward across her desk. "Sister, listen carefully: *You—do—not—know that.* In all your patient logic you've taken your own Lord and Savior entirely out of the equation. You will pray, and I will pray, and Ines and all the children will pray, and God shall hear us and answer."

"And if he doesn't?"

Eustace's grin widened. Just past her lipless mouth Mary glimpsed a row of discolored, nubby teeth. "Death is still an answer, is it not?" Mary's mouth opened in an O of surprise, and still that grin grew, almost transforming itself into a snarl. "It wouldn't be the first answer of its kind at St. Teresa's. I won't have a sister under *my* roof questioning the will of the Father or of myself. *Do I make myself clear?*"

Mary didn't know what to say. Certainly she wouldn't *agree* with this hateful woman. She found herself, instead, rising to her feet, clutching the baby protectively to her, and still without answering Eustace's question she turned and strode from the office.

"Sister Mary Matthew!"

She made it halfway to the stairs before her

willpower was pulled apart like cotton candy and she turned back toward the office. Standing in the middle of the living room, between the couch and a threadbare armchair, Mary saw that the dining table stood empty. Judging from the distant sound of children, she guessed that Ines had elected to serve their charges their breakfast out on the lawn today. Most certainly to avoid their overhearing Sister Funtime getting berated by Sister Killjoy. A spike of shame pierced her for her harsh words to Ines, but she brushed it away, staring expectantly back at Eustace, who stood in her doorway, finally noticing the sudden immaculate state of the place.

"I do not recall asking you to do the maid's chores," Eustace said.

"I do not recall there being a maid on staff," Mary replied.

"Yes, well. Mr. James can't be expected to pay for our every fancy."

"Could that be the true reason we would deny a child basic medical care? Our benefactor's purse strings?"

Eustace made no reply.

"Perhaps I could bring the matter to him," Mary said. "Surely a Good Samaritan such as he wouldn't want a child's death on his hands. Do you happen to know if he'll be visiting soon?"

Again Eustace remained silent. Her face was unreadable.

"Yes. Well." Mary knew it was maybe a little childish to mimic Eustace's pet phrase at her like a parrot, but she was beyond caring. "I best put Luke to sleep and ask God if he could find it in his heart to spare the baby."

Before she could turn and walk away again, Eustace stepped from the doorway. Her movement, slow, clacking steps drawing her closer and closer, had the effect of holding Mary in place. Whatever backbone she may borrow from Dory Chesterton, the fact remained that Mary Matthew was afraid of Sister Killjoy.

Eustace wove between the couch and armchair and stopped inches from her, her bulging eyes unblinking the entire time.

"Do not," she said, her voice low and husky, "attempt to change how I run things here again. Something tells me that you will not be here long enough to make your mark, so save the rest of us the headache." She sniffed and made a face. "It smells of vinegar."

"Cleanliness," Mary replied, "is next to godliness, Sister, is it not?"

And she turned her back on her superior and walked away, half expecting at any moment to feel claws sink into her back.

Mary put Luke in his crib (in the girls' dorm, beside Tabitha's cot) and sat for a while until his fretting subsided to an uneasy sleep. She did not pray for him as she had said she would, but instead returned to her own room, ignoring the sounds of children outside. Ines could take them for a moment or two longer. She just needed to lie down, rest her head, which had been throbbing for a while now.

She saw when she returned that her Bible was now missing from its place atop the dresser. But that was okay. She'd stopped reading it.

VI.

The night air leeched the warmth from her bones. Mary clung her thin, scratchy nightgown to her as she skirted across the expansive lawn like a shadow in the wind. All she heard as she ran was her hitching breaths and thundering heart, thudding in sickly syncopation with her bare feet as they slapped against and slid across the dewy grass.

She gathered her breath after ducking behind the greenhouse. Out of sight of the mansion, but not of the moon: it hung above her as if taunting her for being out of bounds like a schoolgirl; it bathed her in its almost heady light, and she imagined that this was what it felt like to be drunk. Was this the feeling Lizzie and Benjamin had been chasing with the communion wine? She might have to try it sometime. She slapped a hand over her mouth and giggled in surprise at the thought.

But no time to waste: she took one more steadying breath and hurried on through the tiny, sagging gate into the cemetery. She was briefly reminded of her first night trip to this place, newly arrived and pulled by the hand so Ines could share her secret; it sent shame smoldering through her for not sharing her *own* secret. But Ines hadn't wanted to stand up for Luke—Mary couldn't risk her saying no to *this* as well.

Mary was on a mission. She didn't know if it was a mission from God, but she had an idea that it was a mission *against* Sister Killjoy. Which, as far as Mary was concerned, amounted to the same thing.

As she tiptoed through the overgrown cemetery, weaving her way between headstones, Eustace's voice ran on a loop in her head.

Death is still an answer, is it not?

It wouldn't be the first answer of its kind at St. Teresa's.

Mary had always found a strange comfort in cemeteries, as though a congregation of spirits held constant communion for their living loved ones. She often daydreamed—or, rather, Dorothea Chesterton would daydream, Sister Mary Matthew would never spend her time doing such—of what her own plot and headstone would look like. Sunflowers. That was what she had decided. Sunflowers would be the perfect adornment for her grave, so bright and sunny.

But ever since her confrontation—rebuking, more like—earlier today, with those words Eustace uttered . . . *It wouldn't be the first answer of its kind at St. Teresa's* . . . a horrible sensation, a strangling, turgid darkness, had been slowly, inexorably bubbling its way up Mary's insides. Until, lying on her cot, dreading sleep and the dreams that inevitably came with it, she'd felt as if that bubbling darkness were clogging her throat.

Death is still an answer . . . is it not?

Her thoughts had swirled as if at the bottom of a drain, her throat so clogged she could hardly breathe, and the truth—that horrid, horrid truth that some part of her had known the second Eustace uttered those words—had sunk its claws in her back at last.

And now she was here, in the secrecy of midnight, her heart a timpani in her eardrums as she fumbled to light a match in the middle of a decrepit cemetery.

She whispered a little prayer of apology to the headstone's owner as she scraped the match's tip against it. A light cracked into existence, tiny but seeming as bright as a flare in the dark. Quickly she transferred the lit match to the votive candle in her other hand and then held the candle's flickering wick to the face of the headstone.

EZEKIEL
1920

An icy wind cut through the graveyard like a sickle through wheat. The candle sputtered and died. Darkness engulfed her; she fell, shivering so violently that the candle slipped from her fingers, and her back slammed into a headstone behind her. She cried out.

What had she read on the stone? *Ezekiel.* And beneath that, just one number, the previous year, 1920 . . .

But where was the rest? This Ezekiel's last name, his exact dates of birth and death? Or any other salient characteristics he would always be remembered by?

It seemed to Mary that the moon, gibbous and sickly yellow, was laughing at her as she fumbled with numb fingers for the dropped candle. She found nothing but mulched leaves and squirming insects. Again that dark dread surged up her throat: What if Eustace came here in the daylight and discovered the missing votive candle? Would she suspect Mary?

But no, Mary must forget that awful woman. She wasn't the reason for this covert mission, the *children* were. She was here for *Luke*. She was here for Tabitha and Thomas and Hanna and Haley, for Sean and for Bevvy and for all the others, all who came before and would come after. The candle be damned.

She rescued a second matchstick from her nightgown and lit it, using its sparse light to confirm that, yes, EZEKIEL 1920 was indeed all that marked this particular grave. Hurriedly, using all four matches that she'd nicked from the kitchen, she marched between the rows of graves, whispering feverishly what sparse information she could find on their markers.

ISAAC. 1918.

MILLIE & DEBORAH. 1899.

PETER. R.I.P.

RUTH. 19—. The exact year was either defaced or never given in the first place, she could not tell. This angered Mary for an inarticulate but resolute reason, until she saw the next marking:

BABY.

It was this last that finally took the fight out of Mary. She dropped her last match, not caring that her only nightgown was stained with dirt as she crawled between the graves. Her vision blurred; hot, salt-bitter tears choked her. Just one four-letter word: BABY . . . *baby* . . . no family name, not even a Christian name or year or any marking except the most basic of nouns, and yet that one word said so much.

She sat back on the wet, cold earth and bared her face to the moon. Her throat clogged once more with that thick, roiling darkness. She opened her mouth and it rushed out in a low, defeated moan, and she wept bitterly for so many lost souls.

But what did her discovery mean, exactly? Were these the graves of children? Certainly some of them were. But they couldn't *all* be from sickness. Many of the gravestones had no discernible markings, whether from the passage of time or because no name had been carved into the stone in the first place. That ruled out some plague having swept through St. Teresa's, or the graves would look to be the same age.

Mary feared the answer to this mystery more than she'd feared anything in her life.

But she couldn't give up the search out of fear.

Yes, small rebellions were good for the heart, as Sister Ines had taught her. But Mary was beginning to suspect that there were times when larger rebellions were imperative for the soul.

By the time she'd collected herself, cleaning up and covering her tracks as best she could, Mary found comfort in the darkness. But night would not last forever. She would have to be quick with this next, most risky, step of her mission.

The brass knob of Eustace's office door turned silently — a small mercy.

That mercy was snatched away as she eased the door open and its hinges gave an arthritic creak, shockingly loud in the mansion's stillness.

Mary froze, her knuckles a ghostly white as she clutched the doorknob. Seconds ticked by, great trenches of time in between. Not a sound but her own doomed pulse. Still, she waited; still, tense silence. Holding her breath, she widened the opening a few more inches and slipped inside.

Godspeed, Sister, she thought to herself, and dove into the search before her nerves sent her running back to bed. She clicked on a desk lamp that guarded Eustace's workspace —

But there was nothing. The desk was empty.

Mary nearly panicked and bolted, but that one word, BABY, kept her in place. She'd seen several neat piles of paperwork on Eustace's desk, file folders and loose sheaths covered in bold black ink and the older sister's thin, spidery cursive. She'd *swear* she'd seen it, and not just once, but every single time she'd been inside this wretched office.

A filing cabinet, then. Yes, that was it — Eustace was meticulous, left nothing out of place. Mary circled the desk, scanning the walls of the office. No sign of a filing cabinet, but —

"Aha!" Mary whispered, eyes gleaming in triumph.

She knelt and clasped the desk drawer, tucked below and to the left of Eustace's chair. Inside she found it completely empty. She frowned. Something about it seemed off. What was it? She stared inside it for several seconds, then dipped a finger to the bottom and swiped the grainy wood. That was it — no dust. The drawer wasn't only empty; it was pristine. It was very possible that this drawer held all of Eustace's papers but had recently been emptied. A still, small voice in the back of her mind reminded her of all those boxes full of papers down in the basement. Were the answers she sought down there?

Mary closed the drawer. She still remembered the sting of that slap across her face. Eustace's promise to kick her out. No. She was not ready to risk that so soon.

She swiftly checked the other drawers until finally coming to the bottom one on the right side of the chair. At her tug, she was met with a faint *click* and resistance. The drawer was locked. It, like its empty twin, was bigger than the rest, large enough to approximate the space needed to file paperwork. It *had* to be the one.

But where was the key?

Mary rushed around the office, feeling an increasing sense of futility. Eustace was in control here; she always had been. She wouldn't hide a key where a child — or a rebellious nun — would find it. Not in these drawers or that frame or those books. Mary riffled through their pages, she swept a hand beneath the rug, she stood on the chair and unscrewed the light fixture. Nothing.

"God damnit," she breathed — and froze.

As the profane swear left her lips, her gaze had met that of the Virgin Mary figurine at the center of the desk. It had been given pride of place, and now it had front row seats to one of God's faithful servants trespassing and taking her Lord's name in vain. She should not be here — how could she be doing such a thing — she should be . . .

A second time, that still, small voice spoke in the back of her mind.

And suddenly, she knew precisely where to find the key.

Mary reverently lifted the Virgin Mary figurine, icy cold in her clammy hands, and found, tucked just inside an aperture on its underside, a tiny copper key. Of course! Eustace hid it in plain sight, within an expensive-looking figurine of a holy woman whom none of them, not even the children, would dare touch. It was so naïve, Mary now realized. Arrogant, even. How could Eustace expect everyone else to stay perfectly within bounds when she herself was not?

Without another second wasted, Mary bent and unlocked the secret drawer.

Another, final rush of disappointment—it was not a filing cabinet, it did not hold folders of important documents that would help Mary sleuth out the dark history of this place—but then, upon noticing the drawer's actual contents, she perked back up. She'd failed at finding what she came for, but what she *did* find . . . well, perhaps this was a risk worth taking after all. Carefully, she pulled each item from its designated spot inside the drawer.

First, Mary's pocket-size Bible, lovingly worn from her hours upon hours of study. Wrapped around it were her rosary beads, clinking softly together in her hands.

Beneath the Bible was Mary's precious crucifix, still on its necklace chain. The sight of it nearly sent her into a sobbing fit. She loved this crucifix with every fiber of her being, could remember the day she received it two years ago. She'd announced to her parents that she would do what they wanted and give up her silly dream of going to college and instead give her life to Christ; on the day she was to be shipped away, her stern, thunderous father had given her this. The only gift she'd ever received from him. It was made of cheap materials, but it was hers, and she loved it. Oh, how she longed in this moment to tuck it back into her habit, but she knew she could not. To do so would unequivocally amount to a confession.

Also in the drawer was a glass bottle of brown liquid.

Mary's eyes widened in surprise. This was alcohol, and expensive-looking judging by the craftsmanship of the bottle. Bought before the Prohibition, or smuggled across the border? The sloshing liquid had been drained to merely a third of the way up the glass. But what did this mean? Another secret treasure confiscated from a resident, a teenager or possibly a nun? Or . . . Mary glanced up at the figurine on the desk. She had an idea that this particular item in the locked drawer belonged to Eustace herself.

She thought of her trip down to the basement to find more communion wine. The slap across the face that she'd received as punishment. The hypocrisy was almost too much to bear. It tore at the cover protecting Sister Mary Matthew's well of resolve. Before she could let it, before she could think anything further, she twisted off the cap and tilted her head. A shoot of liquid fire blazed down her throat. She coughed, then grinned sheepishly at the Virgin Mary figurine. She'd never tasted hard liquor. It burned; her lips turned numb from its touch. She was reminded of the bleach she'd used to scrub this place clean, and thought of it now scouring the depths of her soul.

She replaced the bottle with shaking hands and came to the last item in the drawer: a locked metal box. A cash box, she thought. When she lifted it, one hand beneath and one hand holding the handle at the top, she could tell that it was very full, perhaps stuffed as full as it allowed. Coins clinked mutedly inside, held mostly in place by whatever bills surrounded them.

A fresh bout of anger prickled her skin as she set the heavy box back inside. The general disrepair and decrepitude of the mansion, the overgrown cemetery, the ratty blankets and clothing for the children, the shortness of staff . . . a desperately ill baby in need of medication . . . and here was the woman put in charge of providing for these children, locking away what was surely a small fortune. This went beyond the behavior of a miser. This . . . this was sin.

This was evil.

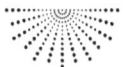

VII

"Sister? What are you doing? Where's Fran?"

Mary glanced over her shoulder briefly before turning back to the kitchen stove. "Good morning, children! Did we remember to say our prayers?"

"Of course we did!" exclaimed Hanna.

"We did!" echoed Haley. "Jesus is going to give us the most *beautiful* day!"

"Beautiful!" Hanna agreed. Again, it came out: *Beau-uuuuutiful!* "But what are you doing in here, Sister Mary?"

"Fran couldn't make it today," Mary explained, scrambling the eggs as they cooked in the pan. "In fact, Sister Ines and I may be making your meals for the fore-seeable future."

In truth, Fran was never coming back. Mary had woken this morning, still foggy from her late night sneaking around the premises, to the sound of crying punctuated with stern, staccato orders. Ines was shaking her awake, listening to the voices herself. She'd explained, in a hurried whisper, that Eustace had just sent the cook packing, accusing her of stealing match-sticks from the kitchen. Mary and Ines, along with their usual duties, would now be in charge of the children's meals as well.

Seemingly satisfied with this answer, the twins turned away, perhaps to share the news with the other children.

"Girls," Mary called, bringing them back. "I wanted to ask you something . . ."

She turned the burner on low and bent to eye level with the two smiling girls, glancing around for eaves-droppers. "I was wondering," she whispered, "if you remembered any other adults coming to visit the orphanage."

In the sobering sunlight streaming through the kitchen windows (which were required to stay closed but were allowed to be uncovered by curtains), Mary had a lot of time to think of the previous night's revelations as she went about preparing breakfast. And one thing that had suddenly occurred to her was that no prospective parents that she knew of had come to visit any of the orphans. But wasn't part of the purpose of St. Teresa's to find adoptive parents for children in need of a proper home?

The twins glanced at each other, eyebrows shooting up in impish curiosity. They cried out together:

"Mr. James!"

Hanna said, "He comes here lots! And I heard" — glancing dramatically around for any sign of Sister Killjoy — "sometimes he brings *candy*."

Haley nodded. "*Cotton* candy."

Mary nodded, mulling this over. "And does he . . . does he bring other adults? To meet the children?"

Haley's little brow pinched up in thought. "I dunno . . . maybe?"

"Maybe," Hanna agreed, "but *I've* never seen them."

Haley nodded. "Just Mr. James. But maybe he *takes* the children to the new parents!"

"So it does happen, then?" Mary asked. "Children *are* adopted?"

The girls beamed in the affirmative. Hanna took her sister's hand and said, "One day Mr. James will take my sister and me to *our* new parents."

"Our new parents, oh, yes," Haley agreed. "Just like he did with Zeke!"

Hanna nodded. "Zeke is with his parents now!"

The girls went skipping away, swinging their clasped hands between them. But Mary didn't move. She was frozen in place, bent over, her mind reeling.

Zeke, they'd said. *Zeke* . . . as in . . .

"Ezekiel," she whispered.

Eventually she stood, staring down at yet not seeing the pan full of burnt scrambled eggs. What she saw was nowhere near this kitchen; what she saw was just a short midnight dash across the lawn, around the greenhouse, and through an ancient gate.

EZEKIEL
1920

It couldn't be helped: she would have to do the unthinkable and risk everything.

She would have to return to the basement.

. . .

FOR HER SECOND excursion to the basement, Mary waited until nightfall. She didn't dare take any more matches, and so ran one hand along the wall, the other clutching to the railing, as she navigated down the basement's black, black throat.

She was exhausted from the previous night's lack of sleep, and after a long day of running a house full of children, even between Ines and herself, it was nearly too much to bear. And now, feeling the dank cold of the basement seep its fingers into her skin and tickle her nose, she was afraid she'd become just as sick as Luke.

But what could she do? She couldn't stop. Not after what she'd learned.

She had to know what was going on at St. Teresa's Joyous Youths Orphanage.

When she reached the bottom of the creaky steps, she found two surprises. First was that there was light down here: the window, a thin strip of dirty glass near the basement's low ceiling, allowed for a slice of buttery moonlight. This was a fortunate stroke of luck. The second surprise, however, was far less fortunate.

Somewhere inside this basement was the steady, sonorous sound — Mary was sure of it — of a living creature's slow, softly ragged breathing.

Mary stood frozen at the bottom of the steps, holding her breath, until her eyesight had adjusted enough to the moonlit gloom. No creature presented itself; only the same cluttered stacks of boxes and crates that she'd found before. Perhaps her ears were playing tricks on her, she reasoned. Surely nothing lived down here. It was the rumble of a boiler, or water streaming through pipes.

She continued on, quickly selecting a few boxes and setting them beneath the window. She'd remembered somewhere in the hours since searching Eustace's office how she'd stumbled upon these boxes during her first trip down to the basement, and sure enough, at last — her heart surged with a moment of tempered triumph! — she'd discovered paper. Stacks and stacks of it. File folders and loose papers and thick, official-looking documents. Newspapers were also abundant. She stared at the papers in her arms, willing her eyes to see better in the dark, but most of it was gibberish to her. Tax forms, maybe, or old, horribly kept bookkeeping. Some of the papers seemed to be for an institution other than an orphanage; words jumped out at her. *Inmate Number. Infraction. Recommended Therapy.* What were these for? Some kind of prison camp? Stranger still were some of the headlines from the newspapers that jumped out at her. She didn't know what to make of all of it. Headlines about missing children and unclaimed land and a New York governor implicated in a money laundering scheme. Surely some invisible thread connected these events, unless the newspapers had been kept for some other, completely benign article not on the front page.

Strewn out across the floor she found large, thick sheets of paper that she thought, beneath the sparse light, were a pretty blue color. Blueprints. At first she thought she'd found the blueprints of St. Teresa's, but on closer inspection she didn't recognize any of the designs. There was the fountain, yes, just like out in front of the mansion, but instead of the schoolhouse and mansion and chapel spread out in a gently curving line the way they did, there was . . . what was that supposed to be, exactly? It looked like — well, it looked like a great big half-moon smile. In fact, if she weren't mistaken, she'd swear that a child had gotten hold of this blueprint paper and scrawled a large cartoony smiling face, and then one of the older kids, or perhaps the architect, had elected to populate the face with geometric structures to cover up the indiscretion. A theater here, an outdoor pavilion here, rows of restaurants, and . . .

She squinted down at the paper. A massive, snaking rollercoaster? And on the opposite side, a Ferris wheel.

What would the orphanage need with blueprints for some elaborate carnival?

It seemed there was writing in the corner, but she found that this part of the blueprint had been ruined with some kind of slick, corrosive mold. On further inspection, she found that the haphazard sheath of blueprints had been resting partly where that stack of boxes had disintegrated during her first trip. The black stain climbing the wall was still there, and it had partially ruined the blueprints.

A snuffling sound echoed out from the far corner of the basement.

Mary spun around, staring into the darkness. The moonlight did not penetrate far enough for her to distinguish shapes or movement. Had she imagined it?

There it was again: an animal's disgruntled snort.

So, no, she hadn't imagined it. This was the source of the steady breathing sounds she'd heard when she first came down.

Her breath quickened. She wasn't alone down here.

Not quite ready to give up on this quest, but not knowing what else to do, Mary reminded herself of that tough stuff she was made of—bleach, vinegar, lye—and she began taking tentative, catlike steps toward the darkest part of the basement. Perhaps more answers lay that way.

The creature's breathing grew louder with every step. *No. Stop. Come back.*

She paused. There was that still, small voice again, whispering in the back of her mind. Only this time . . . this time, she could have sworn it didn't actually come from the back of her mind, but from *behind* her.

Don't go over there, the voice said. *Danger!*

What in the hell was happening down here? Mary wondered.

Come back, the voice whispered. *Come to me, Dory.*

That name was like an untethering. At the sound of it, she felt some old part of her that had been hiding itself somewhere deep within her heart come peek its head out, suddenly desperate to be seen. Dory . . . twenty-year-old Dorothea Annabeth Chesterton of Syracuse, New York. It felt like a lifetime ago since she'd thought of herself as little fun-loving Dory. The name took some of the urgency out of her mission—it made her want to run as fast as she could to sunlight, to smiles, to singing children and popping popcorn and raucous laughter, as fast as her feet could take her.

She turned back toward the basement window and retraced her steps.

Yes, whispered the voice. *Welcome, welcome, welcome . . . Dory . . .*

The voice led her, both surprisingly and somehow not surprising at all, to that large dark stain climbing the wall. Or, no, to where the stain spread in a wide circle on the floor, to what lay at its center as if placed there for some kind of ritual.

"You!" Mary breathed.

The beautiful crucifix. She remembered finding it during her search for the communion wine. It was the only item in the entire stack of boxes that the stain hadn't seeped through to the point of disintegration. If anything, it looked as if someone had given it a good, loving polish. She loved the detailed carving work of the two beams that made the cross—such intricate designs for such a small crucifix, about the length and width of her flattened hand. And the pitiful, angular scarecrow figure of Christ in perpetual crucified pose, with those perfectly cut rubies glinting bloodily up from his palms and feet and dripping from his thorny crown. Those ocean-blue sapphires set into Christ's face, faceted like the eyes of a fly, winking up out of the dark as if Jesus himself were about to share a secret with lowly Dory Chesterton.

I've been calling to you in your dreams, Dory . . .

The figurine's thorn-crowned head, impossibly, swiveled from where it rested against the cross, and Mary's throat went dry as Christ's mouth stretched and tapered up at the corners. He was *grinning* at her.

. . . oh, Dory, please don't leave me down here again!

Mary's heart thundered, her breath hitching, and bright spots of light wheeled in her vision like a nightmarish carousel spinning out of control. Had she fallen on her head? Had she inhaled hallucinatory fumes from whatever black mold this stain was?

You of all people, Jesus said, *trying to explain away a miracle?*

"I . . ." she muttered, dizzy and drunken and terrified. "I . . . I—"

Quiet. You'll wake the monster.

Somehow, Mary knew that he was talking about whatever lay behind her in the depths of the basement.

Dory—forgive me—Sister Mary, Jesus said, his crazed

grin somehow stretching wider than his face. *I've been waiting for you. The children have been waiting. We need you, Mary. This orphanage needs you. Will you not help us? Do you not love us?*

Mary stared down at the crucifix resting in her outstretched palms. She did not recall picking it up, but here it was, surprisingly yet pleasantly cool to the touch. She could not believe what she was seeing . . . but, then again, couldn't she? Sure, in all of imaginative Dory Chesterton's wildest dreams she hadn't expected such a thing as this, but that did not mean she did not believe in miracles. Miracles were precisely what appealed to her most about giving herself to Christ. And what greater way to do exactly that than to rescue him from this dreary, evil-fouled basement?

Eyes gleaming in the moonlight, a dazed, almost bovine expression slackening her jaw, Sister Mary Matthew gazed lovingly down at her Savior and whispered:

"Tell me what to do, my Lord."

VIII.

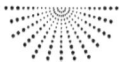

*S*unday morning — the best morning of them all! — arrived in a herald of sparkling sunshine, bathing the earth in God's glory, and Sister Mary Matthew never felt so rapturously *alive*. She flitted around the kitchen like a fairy-tale princess, dancing along to the sounds of birdsong through the flung-wide kitchen windows, humming some infectious little ditty she had no memory of learning.

"Welcome, welcome, welcome . . ."

Bacon — she'd found a hunk of it secreted away in the very bottom of the ice box — sizzled on the pan, flinging up flecks of grease. Her habit had never felt lighter, like silk pajamas flowing about her, her hair glistening as if with a halo. She felt like a Hollywood movie star — Gloria Swanson, losing herself in her new leading role as the angelic nun come to save the orphan children from the doldrums of apathetic torpor and whisk them away into musical numbers and happily-ever-afters.

"Come on inside, smile wide, and . . ."

"Sister?"

She spun around to find Sister Ines Joseph standing at the kitchen entrance, a look of puzzled bewilderment on her beautiful face.

"Sister!" Mary squealed, practically falling into her fellow nun's arms.

Ines caught her out of reflex and obliged in the embrace, then pulled her back to inspect her at arm's length. She reached a finger up to Mary's temple and came away with a spot of blood. So many questions danced in her eyes, and when she finally asked one, it came out as a single word: "Breakfast?"

"Oh, yes!" Mary pulled away, returning to the pan of bacon. "It's Sunday, the most important day of all! The Lord may rest on the seventh day, but the children have church. Got to make sure they're well fed and ready for the day."

"Yes . . . I only meant, we'd agreed to split the cooking duties between the two of us. You cooked the meals only yesterday—"

"Oh, Ines, my dear, do not worry yourself one bit. Alllllll taken care of!"

"You seemed so tired—"

"Yes, and you know?" Mary shot a serious look over her shoulder at Ines. "I wanted to apologize for being so distracted. What a *burden* this place must be for you without my help! But I've prayed, I've rested, I've listened to my Savior, and from now on I am with you from morning till night." She grinned as if at some shared joke. "Well—except for our personal prayers, of course."

"I . . . I . . ."

Mary turned again to Ines, seeing the halting expression on her face. She seemed unsure of herself, so unlike the Sister Ines Joseph she'd come to know and love. "Why, Sister, what is it? Whatever could be wrong?"

Ines broke eye contact. Her breathing hitched. "I am the one who should be apologizing, I . . . I did not have the children's best interest at heart. I should have gone with you to Eustace about Luke's illness." One fat tear spilled from her thick lashes.

"Oh, my sweet, sweet Ines, please!" Mary stepped to her for another embrace. "Do not think another moment on it. I know *I* haven't. The important thing is that Luke is still with us. You were right, anyway. *Eustace* was right, and I'm not so proud as to deny that. As long as we pray, the Lord will provide."

Ines allowed herself a single gasping intake of breath, sobbing into Mary's habit, before straightening and stepping away, a mixture of relief and embarrassment in her voice. "Yes. You are right, of course, praise him." Her eyes, suddenly curious, followed Mary as she returned to her cooking. "You . . . I thought I felt something, Sister. Beneath your habit?"

But Mary seemed not to hear the question. Instead, she burst into action setting the dining table for breakfast. It was a tight fit, but she managed to find a place for all the children old enough to enjoy their meal at table. She finished placing breakfast — fluffy scrambled eggs, crisp strips of bacon, fresh cow's milk, and orange slices — upon the tablecloth just in time to give another squeal of delight and welcome the children as they began to trickle down the stairs, yawning.

The first to notice the food was Adam, a ten-year-old from among Ines's charges, and at his cry of "Bacon!" they all came rushing for a seat. Mary served up the food, complimenting each of the children and asking them what they most looked forward to in their day. At one point, she snatched a bacon strip from Lizzie's plate and curled it in front of her face in the shape of a smile. She was skipping around the table, singing that the only rule at St. Teresa's was to never stop smiling, and at some point among the chorus of giggles a chant was taken up—

"Sister Funtime! Sister Funtime! Sister Funtime!"

—when Sister Agatha Eustace stormed into the room.

All fell still. One of the littles—two-year-old Sean, sitting on an older girl's lap—began a preemptive whimper in expectation of Eustace's wrath.

"Good morning, Sister!" Mary exclaimed, beaming unashamedly at the older woman, the errant bacon strip still raised in one hand. "Care for some breakfast before church? I was telling the children how much they will love today's Sunday school lesson. I hope you don't mind, but I got a burst of inspiration during my morning prayers and planned it all out. We shall be learning about . . ." She grinned around at the children as if about to reveal that Santa was coming early this year. ". . . Jonah and the whale and the importance of obedience!"

Eustace greeted this proclamation with several halting seconds of silence. She merely stared around in bewilderment, taking in the table full of food, the giggling children, the open windows, and, most of all, Sister Mary Matthew herself.

Finally, she spoke: "Very good, Sister. I look forward to your lesson."

She gave a curt nod that could almost be interpreted as grudging approval, then turned on her heel, the fabric of her heavy habit snapping behind her, and left.

There followed several more moments of silence in which the children all stared wide-eyed after her, then back at Mary, then all around at each other. The chant began again, slower now, a playful, excited whisper:

"Sis-ter Fun-time . . . Sis-ter Fun-time . . . Sis-ter Fun-time!"

All the while, all through breakfast and on through Sunday school, Sister Mary smiled wider than she'd ever smiled before. Everything around her—the children, Ines, the orphanage, the sunshine—was muted as if behind a giant bubble. The center of her world was just beneath her habit, resting against her breast. It hung from a braid of her own hair, yanked free from her temple at the roots and woven into a necklace.

From this hung the crucifix, with Jesus and his sapphire eyes, pulsing hotly and drowning out the sound of her own heart.

Tell me what to do, my Lord.

She'd uttered those words only hours before, but it seemed to Mary a lifetime ago. The conversation that followed, down in the dark depths of the basement, was like a bottomless trench, forever separating her life as Dorothea Annabeth Chesterton of Syracuse, New York, and her life as Sister Mary Matthew of St. Teresa's Joyous Youths Orphanage.

He'd told her exactly what to do, oh yes he had indeed, and it lit a fire of clarity within her that cleansed her soul. A baptism by fire. A spotlight, cutting through the black void and illuminating the path she must take.

Indeed, that trench separating her old life from this new one was so deep, so impenetrable, that she could not remember now anything that had been said. She only recalled before — whispering down to him, "Tell me what to do, my Lord" — and after. Once he'd told her what to do, she left the basement. She did not give her reason for coming down there in the first place another thought. Why waste precious time rooting through old files and forms and newspapers and blueprints when she now held in the palm of her hand the all-seeing, all-knowing Christ?

Once she'd safely returned to her room, he had whispered into her mind:

Close the door.

She'd paused. "We are to keep the doors to our private quarters open at all times."

Though there was no light to reflect off of them, Jesus's sapphire eyes flashed brightly up at her. He said again:

Close the door.

She swung it shut without another word or hesitation, berating herself.

Inside, with no light but those flashing sapphires and no sound but that of her blood being pumped through her body, his voice came again:

Part the curtains.

Again, she paused, and before she could stop herself she began, "Sister Eustace says that we are to keep — "

The curtains flapped apart, their metal rings screaming along the rod.

Is Sister Killjoy the master of this house or am I?!

The thought slammed into the back of her head like the dull blade of a hatchet. She stumbled to the window, falling in her haste, slamming a shoulder into the sill. Steadying herself on her knees, she wrenched the thick black curtains farther apart. She nearly cried out at the brightness of the moonlight as it hit her face.

I cannot do everything alone, he said, his voice calm once more. *Just parting those curtains after so much time trapped in the basement has sapped my strength. I need you.*

Those last few words sent a thrill through her.

Let me drink in the moon.

Shoulder smarting with every movement, Mary placed the crucifix on the windowsill so that Jesus lay on his back. The full moon grinned down from the night sky. Jesus's sapphire eyes seemed to spin where they lay, glowing in the light streaming through the windowpane.

This is where I shall spend my nights, he told her. *I spent far too long hidden away in that basement, and I must recoup my strength.*

Grateful that she need only part the curtains at night, and thus could avoid Eustace's wrath, Mary whispered, "Yes, my Lord."

But I cannot be allowed to see the sun, lest its far stronger light damage my wood, he continued. *You must carry me on your person at all times during the day. You mustn't let another soul learn of my existence. I shall take the place of that cheap crucifix of yours, the one Killjoy confiscated.*

"Yes, my Lord."

If I am to be worn around your neck, tucked against the flesh over your heart, you will need a necklace.

"I have none, my Lord." Her cheeks flushed with shame.

Already giving up? This from the same Sister Funtime who made a game for the children from no more than an old bicycle tire and a discarded tree branch? Surely you can think of something. Something worthy of my sacrifice . . .

Her face still burned as her mind raced. His sapphire eyes seemed to penetrate deep inside her soul, plucking the solution like fruit from a tree. She felt the thought like a decoupling, something physically pruned from her brain, excavated, and brought to hover before her mind's eye. Yes. Of course!

He smiled. *Just a taste, child. You shall see all by my side.*

Her eyes glistened wetly. She nodded. Eyes forever on him, she reached up to her scalp and with slow, deliberate movements wrapped a thick cord of her hair once, twice, around her fist.

"This necklace," she intoned, "shall be but a single drop of my sacrifice."

She gripped the windowsill with this same fist and, eyes still on her Savior, yanked her head back. The cord of hair remained wrapped around her clenched hand, having ripped itself from her head by the roots. Her scalp sang sharply with bright, sunshiny pain. Without pause, she began pulling the individual strands apart and braiding them into a makeshift necklace.

Jesus, on his cross, smiled up at her in the moonlight.

From her temple dripped a single blood-red ruby.

IX

*S*everal days later, Sister Eustace made another rare appearance at breakfast to make an announcement. Later that very day, St. Teresa's beneficent benefactor, Mr. James, would be stopping by for a visit. Mary would have thought this would send the children into a fit of excited whispers about one or all of them possibly getting adopted (or, at the very least, Haley and Hanna exclaiming about cotton candy), but instead the announcement was greeted by absolute silence and then one sharp intake of breath.

Eustace turned to the person who had gasped. "Is there something wrong, Sister Ines Joseph?"

Ines, in a moment uncharacteristic to her usual boisterous joviality, avoided eye contact. She stared down and muttered, "No, Sister. It's just that, uh . . . well, you see, the sister and I had planned to take the children to the blackberry patch today."

Eustace narrowed her eyes, glancing at Mary as if for confirmation. Mary kept her face neutral, but she was certain that Ines had never mentioned blackberries to her, either today or ever before. Were they even in season?

"I see," the older sister said. "Unusual to go during the school week, is it not?"

Ines faltered at this, so Mary spoke up in a burst of inspiration: "We thought it a good chance for a field trip. To witness the wonders of nature is to see the wisdom of God, don't you think?"

Eustace considered this briefly. "Yes. Well. We can't very well show our gratitude toward the good Mr. James if he arrives to an empty house, now, can we? This field trip can wait another day."

"Oh, but, Sister," Ines said, barely hiding the panic in her eyes, "you are right, of course — Mr. James deserves to be showered with our gratitude. At least allow, please, for Sister Mary to go to the blackberry patch. I can handle all the household duties while she is away, and she'll be able to return just in time to send off Mr. James with a basket of fresh fruit!"

Perhaps she thought this a grand idea; perhaps she enjoyed the fact that this would effectively make any field trip with the children unnecessary. Regardless, Sister Eustace agreed to Ines's proposal and carried on with preparations for the day's visitor. As they bustled about, cleaning up breakfast, Mary could see the relief in Ines. In all the hurry, though, she did not get a chance to ask what it meant.

MARY DID NOT HAVE the shoes for trekking into the wilderness, but she was grateful for the chance to have some alone time with her Savior. He throbbed against the flesh between her breasts, hidden from the sunlight as commanded, and whispered to her. She reveled in every blister that raised itself on the soles of her feet, every line of sweat that itched her scalp and salted her skin, each another drop to fill her well of sacrifice.

She wondered aloud, "Why was Ines so insistent I collect blackberries today?"

It's not the blackberries, he responded, his tone that of an impatient father explaining the obvious to a dimwitted child. *She wanted you away during the visit.*

"From our benefactor?"

Perhaps she wanted him all to herself.

Mary paused, resting one hand against the bark of a tree.

Perhaps she feels threatened by the new, popular sister.

Mary blushed. "Who, silly little Dory?"

The one the children call Sister Funtime.

She couldn't deny that the residents of St. Teresa's shared a love for Sister Mary Matthew—even Eustace had changed her tune recently. Ines, on the other hand, seemed to slowly shrink down from the care-free, rebellious sister who showed Mary to her room all those weeks before. Lately she was hesitant, quiet; Mary could not recall the last time she'd heard that sleigh-bell laugh she so loved. Jesus must be right. This blackberry errand was just a guise for Ines's desire to keep Mr. James all to herself.

Mary continued deeper into the forest, following the path someone had marked with strings tied around the trunks of trees. Very well. She would give Ines her time in the spotlight. There was nothing Mary enjoyed more than one-on-one time with the smiling Savior tucked against her skin.

. . .

WHEN SHE RETURNED, her wicker basket was practically spilling with blackberries—indeed a bit past ripe, some already withering from the fast-approaching cold weather. A few had stained the inside of her mouth a midnight blue. She'd barely managed to cross the lawn when Ines burst from the kitchen's back door in a panic.

"Sister, what—"

"Thomas!" Ines exclaimed. "He's gone! No one can find him."

"Oh, I'm sure he's merely wandered off. You know how he is."

"No, you don't understand, Mary." She clutched at Mary's habit, her voice turning to a whisper. *"Mr. James is asking after him."*

Mary gently pressed the basket of berries toward Ines until she took it in her arms. "Take these inside and wash a small basketful for our visitor. I'll find our little escapee, don't you worry."

None of what she said seemed to dissipate the atmosphere of worry swirling in Ines's eyes, but she did as she was told and disappeared through the door.

Mary turned toward the lawn.

Behind the greenhouse.

The sun was just kissing the tops of the trees. It was still too early to bring Jesus out from his hiding place, but he did not need to be shown their surroundings to tell her where little Thomas had run off to.

Mary's smile, which had never left even in the face of the other sister's panic, grew wider as she strolled back across the expanse of grass. Past the greenhouse and around its far wall, she spotted the cemetery gate, open and moving slightly back and forth on its rusty hinges.

Through it and past the first few rows of headstones she came across a whimpering, cowering child.

"Thomas?"

The boy turned to her, eyes wide with fright. His hands and knees were grubby with dirt, as well as one cheek where he'd swiped away a streak of tears.

Her brow furrowed. This wasn't the usual bumbling disappearing act he performed every few days. This was a frightful retreat.

She bent down. "Thomas . . . what's wrong, sweet boy?"

Fresh tears poured down, mixing with the dirt and his boogers. He leapt forward, burying his face in Mary's bosom. Before she could wrap her own arms around him, however, he gave a muffled yelp and fell back, staring at her habit as if it had bit him.

"Look at me, Thomas. Up here. That's right, good. Now, deep breaths. It's okay. Sister Funtime's got you now. Would you give Sister Funtime a smile? No? But Thomas . . . do you remember the one rule of St. Teresa's?"

Another strange difference in Thomas's behavior: he was inconsolable. Tickling fingers to his little belly did nothing but make him squirm and pout. He wouldn't join her in song. He wouldn't smile. None of her Sister Funtime antics penetrated his fear. Usually the boy was so easy to distract, so quick to a fit of laughter that would wipe his worries clear from his mind.

She gave up, slumping against the headstone beside him. "What is it? Tell me, Thomas. Confess right now."

He sniffed, his head drooping between his shoulders for a moment, giving her a clear view of the letters etched into the stone just behind him —

EZEKIEL
1920

—and finally he said, "He's . . . he's a meanie . . ."

Her Savior's insistent whisper: *Sister Agatha Eustace will be a meanie too if you do not take this child inside immediately.*

"A meanie?" she asked. "Did one of the older boys pick on you, Thomas? Was it Benjamin?"

But before the boy could answer, Jesus said, *I will not be ignored!*

The wood of his cross burned like a smoldering coal against her flesh. There came the smell of charred fabric.

Mary jumped into action, biting down the pain. Thomas threw himself into a tantrum in her arms, and halfway across the lawn she had to set him down. He almost escaped, but paused at the sound of an automobile engine coughing itself awake.

"Well, now you've done it," Mary said, for once letting frustration at a child seep into her voice. "Mr. James was asking after you, but now he'll be leaving. Sister Agatha Eustace will be sending you to bed without supper."

But the boy did not seem to regret his actions. He let her get a better grip and sling him across one shoulder. It smarted beneath the toddler's little body, but again she ignored the pain, focusing on the residual heat of the now cooling crucifix to clear her mind.

"I follow your command, my Lord," she said, smiling, and entered the back door of the orphanage.

. . .

St. Teresa's Joyous Youths Orphanage was anything but joyous on her return from the blackberry patch. Its residents seemed deeply out of sorts, but none of them were talkative about what was bothering them. Ines was nowhere to be seen, the children were despondent and barely touched their dinner, and Eustace seemed to have forgotten her recent approval of the youngest sister, scolding Mary for her extended absence and disappearing into her office.

Unsure what else to do, Mary put the children to bed early and retreated to her own room. She paused at the threshold, frowning. Sister Ines's room sat beside her own, and its door, despite Eustace's strict rules, was closed. Just loud enough to be heard through the thin wall separating their rooms was the other sister's muffled sobs.

Mary whispered toward the closed door, "Sister . . . ?"

The sobs stopped. A moment of silence, then shuffling from inside, and the door cracked open. In the shadows, Ines's face looked strange. Mary stepped closer and gasped.

"What is it, Mary?" Ines mumbled. Her words were thick with mucus.

"Your face," Mary breathed.

Sister Ines inclined her head so that more shadows shrouded her. Bruises like blackberry juice stains kissed her skin. One eye was swollen shut, and blood beaded from a crack on her lower lip, reopened from speaking.

"It's not so bad in daylight, I'm sure." Ines tried to laugh, but the sleigh bells refused to sound. "I need my rest, Sister. Goodnight."

The door closed.

Mary stood there, dumbfounded. Her heart ached for her friend. She wished to comfort her, to climb into her bed and swaddle her and rock her to sleep. She reached for the doorknob.

You've harmed her enough, don't you think? came that still, small voice.

Mary's face heated with shame as she snatched her hand away. She retreated instead to her own room, closing the door behind her as she'd come to do every night. The quiet sobs resumed just on the other side of the wall. As she knelt before the window, sweeping the curtains free of the sill, Mary whispered, "Do you think that I'm the one to blame for this?"

Remember who you are speaking with. I do not think it. I know it.

Her fingers trembled as she pulled the braided necklace from around her neck and set the crucifix on the windowsill. The moon's light glimmered in the rubies on his palms. They reminded her of the blood beading on Ines's plump bottom lip.

You stupid girl, Jesus went on. *Who do you think did that to her? Whether it was at the hand of Sister Killjoy or her Good Samaritan, who do you think guided that hand?*

"I . . . I don't understand . . ."

Mr. James wished to see one of the children he provides for. Ines was headed out to find the boy when you stopped her. You certainly took your time with the child once I led you to his hiding place. The boy was disobedient, and so were you when I told you to take him inside. Sister Funtime delayed the boy's return, didn't she, and by then it was too late and our visitor had left. You did this to her, Dory. Foolish, stupid, silly little Dory.

"No," she whispered. A tear fell down one cheek.

No? My, you are *rebellious today.*

Ines's voice chimed in her head—*Small rebellions are good for the heart, Sister*—and she cringed. That bruised and bloody face flashed through her mind. This was no small rebellion. She never should have agreed to the blackberry excursion. Should have stayed and helped with their visitor, should have kept an eye on Thomas and his penchant for wandering off. Shouldn't have dallied so long in the blackberry patch, just like she dallied in the cemetery with the child.

"I'm sorry, my Lord." More tears fell.

His eyes flashed up at her. *It is not me you should apologize to. It is not Ines, nor is it Thomas or James or anyone else. It is your own soul you must make penance to.*

She nodded, gleaning the meaning of his words. As he lay there, bathing in the moonlight, she carefully pushed the windowpane until it juddered up in its frame. An opening of a few inches presented itself beneath the window. The night air stole inside, lighting up her tear-stained cheeks with its cold bite. But she'd found her answers now. She was not Dory. That silly little girl was no more. She was Sister Mary Matthew, and Sister Mary Matthew was perfectly calm as she placed the fingers of her left hand beneath the open window. Before she could reach out her other hand to close the window, her Savior did it for her. His sapphire eyes flashed and spun on his grinning face. The windowpane crashed down in its frame, willed to by her Lord.

Mary swallowed her scream as her fingers, like kindling, snapped.

When she could speak again, she whispered, "Thank you, my Lord."

X.

*T*he nightmares had not visited Mary since she'd taken the crucifix from the basement. But on this night, after hours of lying awake trying to ignore the throbbing ache of her left hand, she found herself suddenly on the green lawn behind the orphanage. It was bright as day, and she was naked. She slapped her hands over her breasts, ashamed, and discovered that her entire body was sticky with blackberries, their juice making her skin appear as bruised as Ines's face. She looked up—

"WELCOME, WELCOME, WELCOME, SISTER FUNTIME!"

—and she screamed. The moon had come so close to the earth that it filled the entire sky, blinding her with ethereal moonlight. It spun, a pockmarked pinwheel, and it grinned down on her. It sang her name. Where the orphanage should have stood there was a massive roller-coaster, constructed out of what appeared to be hundreds of life-size wooden crosses, as if plucked from some seventeenth-century Puritan witch hunt. The rollercoaster's train screamed along its tracks, stone grating on wood. Mary pressed her sticky hands over her ears, but she felt it in her bones: the train was built from heavy tombstones, lined up in a row, gray and cracked and crumbling and thundering along. The children of St. Teresa's rode the rollercoaster with their arms lifted at odd angles, giving the impression that they were strung up across the headstones like Jesus on his cross. The children screamed and laughed in raucous delight, singing along with the moon as they hurtled beneath it—

"WELCOME, WELCOME, WELCOME, SISTER FUNTIME!"

—and Mary screamed back that they would be okay, that she'd save them, and she ran around the roller-coaster, toward where the fountain may or may not be, until she found the operating booth. Her bare feet slapped across the wooden planks of the ramp leading up to it, leaving blackberry footprints bleeding into the grain. She stopped short of the operating booth, however, and slapped her hands once more over her naked breasts and exposed crotch. There was already someone in the booth, hands dancing over the lit controls. She couldn't focus on whoever it was, like looking directly at a solar eclipse only to find yourself staring into the impossible void of a black hole. Some-where in all that black she thought she saw a bright, sunny smiling face, and in a cartoonish voice it sang along with the screaming children—

"WELCOME, WELCOME, WELCOME, SISTER FUNTIME!"

—and it turned all its attention on her, its smile growing lecherous as it gazed down at her nakedness. A slug of a tongue whipped around, wetting its smile. Still she couldn't look directly at it, and in her peripherals it extended one hand, as if inviting her to join it in the operating booth. In that moment she knew, without a shadow of a doubt, that it was either her or the children. There was no saving everyone. But the choice was easy. It was easy for Mary, and it would have been just as easy for Dory. Without hesitation, Sister Funtime lowered her arms from covering her body, stepped forward, and accepted her fate.

MARY WOKE DRENCHED IN SWEAT.

Someone was crying. Ines? She remembered her bloody face peering through the crack in the door, that split lip . . . She raised a hand to her face in sympathy and was met by a sudden violent stab of pain as her fingers brushed the thin blanket. Her body shuddered; a whimper vibrated in her throat.

Oh. *She* was the one crying. She'd wept in her sleep. From the nightmare? Or from —

Last night flooded back to her: what happened *after* a banged-up Ines peered through the crack in the door . . . her Savior's cutting words about her being responsible for Ines's pain . . . guiding the window open, placing her fingers across its threshold like that of a guillotine . . . the window slamming down in its frame . . . *crack* . . . falling asleep with the bones of her hand cradled in her lap as if it were a bird with broken wings.

But she'd done it. She'd taken her penance and done as her Lord commanded. In the bright light of day, his argument for her sin felt less solid, more brittle. But she mustn't think that way.

In the bright light of day . . . ?

She sat bolt upright. The window! The curtains were still thrown wide from last night, and streaming through the glass pane was the midmorning sun.

She'd slept too late.

She rushed about, mortified at all her indiscretions that will have come to light: the closed door, the opened curtains, skipping her morning prayers and various duties to her charges. Surely Eustace will have discovered each of these by now?

When she burst from her room, she stopped, even more disoriented at what she saw out here: the door to Ines's room was also still closed. But what could this mean? Did both Mary and Ines shirk their duties this morning? And if that were the case, why had no one come to ask after them?

She rushed through the mansion, that bubbling dread rising in her throat. Not a creature stirred, not downstairs nor upstairs. Each children's ward stood empty, as did the nursery, kitchen, and main living area downstairs. Signs of breakfast littered the sink and dining table, but otherwise it was as if all inhabitants at St. Teresa's had vanished. As if Mr. James had already returned and whisked them away in his coughing car.

Mary briefly considered the basement door. Something down there seemed to call to her in the mansion's emptiness, some malevolent presence—perhaps that creature she'd heard slumbering in the basement's shadowy depths?

But no, surely the children were not down there. She didn't dare think it.

Outside, the chapel and greenhouse were both similarly empty. She checked the schoolhouse near last; she'd rarely been inside it being the caretaker of the youngest children.

" —renamed it 'New York' just two years before, in 1664."

Lizzie, standing at the front of the classroom, stopped talking when she saw Mary enter at the back of the class. Mary gazed around in wonder. It seemed that every child at the orphanage was in this room, and several of the older kids sat with squirming littles. Haley and Hanna, unlike the other under-fives, sat at the very front and center of the rows of desks, their backs primly straightened, hands steepled before them, soaking in every word of Lizzie's lesson.

"Class," Lizzie said, "please turn to chapter ten and read quietly from your books."

The teenage girl walked down an aisle between the desk rows and met Mary at the schoolhouse's entrance. Before Mary could say anything, Lizzie whispered, her face etched with adult concern, "How's Ines?"

Mary blinked. Again, that bruised face, the split lip, the muffled sobs, those falsely dismissive words — *It's not so bad in daylight, I'm sure* — flashed into her mind.

Misinterpreting her expression, Lizzie added, "Sister Killjoy doesn't know we were left alone this morning. She hasn't appeared yet, and she probably won't till tomorrow. We've, uh, done this before. Things are always a little out of sorts the day after a visit from Mr. James."

Mary focused her thoughts, went over what Lizzie had just said. "You know what happened to Sister Ines?"

"Yes." Lizzie's face paled. "I heard it — we *all* heard it. And I saw the aftermath."

Aftermath. Mary had seen and heard plenty too—that bruised face, those broken sobs—and her own aftermath included a scolding from her Lord, bone-shattering penance, and nightmares. At the thought, her left hand instinctively raised to her chest. She couldn't stop herself from wincing when her mangled fingers pressed against the fabric of her habit, out of the physical pain of her shattered hand. And then the psychological panic at the realization that there was nothing strung around her neck.

In her hurry, she'd left the crucifix sitting on the windowsill.

Lizzie saw the wince. "You couldn't escape him either, huh?"

But the words barely reached her. Her heart raced at what she'd done. With a quick "Please continue with your lessons," she turned and rushed from the schoolhouse, nearly skidding in the gravel outside. She circled along the path to the kitchen back door, her heart speeding faster and faster with every step.

She paused in the hallway leading to her room. Why, she wondered, hadn't he called out to her? The schoolhouse was only just next door; such a distance must be nothing in the eyes of Jesus Christ. Why hadn't he woken her the second rays of sunlight peeked through the window? *I cannot be allowed to see the sun, lest its light damage my wood*—hadn't that been what he'd said?

She tiptoed inside her room, her thoughts a maelstrom of confusion. The curtains were closed, and just beneath their fringe a corner of the crucifix poked out. Carefully, she lifted the black fabric from where it had pooled on the sill and revealed his thin, exposed form.

"My Lord . . . ?"

He did not respond. Nor did his sapphire eyes reflect

the sun. Just inert stones in a detailed yet showy carving of a sickly man nailed to a cross. It was as if he had died.

"My Lord . . ." She fell to her knees, resting her head on the sill. Tears spilled from her eyes. "Please . . . come back. Come back to me."

Again, she remembered his warning: *I cannot see the sun, lest its light damage my wood.* This was all her fault. Once again, she was to blame for another's pain, another's injury. She'd come here to serve her God but instead was responsible for his suffering. Now he'd left her.

That, in her opinion, was the least of what she deserved.

"PLEASE FORGIVE ME, O Lord. Please have mercy on my soul. Please shed all your grace and love on my sister, Ines Joseph, and spare none for myself, who is unworthy. Your wisdom and guidance have brought me this far, miles away from the sinful world, have shed me of my worldly name and given me a purpose from on high, yet I have repaid this with the bumbling stupidity of a foolish and silly little girl. Please, O Lord . . ."

The unyielding floorboards creaked as they pressed bruises into Mary's knees. The gloom of her room—now with both the curtains and the door closing her off from the rest of the world—sent chills into her aching bones. With each prayerful sentence uttered, she clenched her hands together just beneath her bowed head and feverishly whispering lips, sending bright flashes of incandescent pain juddering through her prostrate body. It felt as if the marrow in her fingers had turned to boiling sludge, as if her nerve endings had become pincushions for thousands of needle-thin bone fragments. It was the single most painful thing she'd ever experienced, and she reveled in every moment of it.

Once she had accepted that her Savior had left her, had possibly been driven out of the crucifix by the heat of the sun, Mary turned to prayer. She'd been in this position, kneeling on the floor and pressing herself into the cot, the crucifix laid before her, for what must have been hours. She'd been vaguely aware of the sound of Ines finally opening her own door, though she did not open Mary's to ask after her. Sometime after that, the sounds of children returned to the mansion, but again no one disturbed her. She did not stop praying. She felt cored out, and thought of this prayer as a spiritual shellacking, a way of varnishing her soul against further stain. Each word was bleach, was vinegar and lye, and she would not relent until the grime of her sin had been scoured away.

As she prayed, she carefully examined each indiscretion before moving to the next. Her disobedience under Sister Agatha Eustace, her failure to do her part beside Sister Ines Joseph. Her many doubts and fears. Her failed effort to reach her Heavenly Father in her daily prayers and her subsequent abandonment of further attempts. The days and weeks that had passed since she'd read from her scriptures. Then, finally, her most recent sins: leaving the crucifix in the sun, not bringing Thomas to see Mr. James immediately, going berry-picking against Eustace's better judgment. And Luke: how she'd tried to turn to doctors and man-made medicine rather than do as Eustace had ordered.

At this last, her eyes shot open. A pain-grimacing smile. She had it! She knew what must be done. God, in all his wisdom, had shown her the way simply by virtue of the act of prayer.

She burst forth, barely noticing the pain shooting through her body, and ran from her room. The sound of utensils clinking against plates reached her. She found the others at the dining table, the children and Ines, all pausing in their meal to stare at her in alarm.

She grinned at them in triumph, exclaiming, "We must fast!"

When no one moved, she repeated the words, sweeping around the table to tell them all. "We must fast! For Luke! For the baby! We must pray and we must fast, children, and the Lord will provide the rest—but *we must do our part.*"

Still, no one moved. The children avoided her eyes, staring down at their plates. Ines did not speak up either, and oh, Mary saw now that Ines had not spoken true: her face *was* so bad in daylight; indeed, it was worse. Some of the bruises had already turned a sickening yellow and green, and her bottom lip had swollen to such a size that it was a wonder that she could eat at all.

"Don't you see?" Mary cried, dancing around the table. "It's the only way. The Lord shall save our dear baby boy if he sees our desire, our faith. We fast!"

One of the littles—Sean, sitting on Adam's lap—plucked a green bean from his plate and brought it to his mouth. Mary shrieked and lunged across the table. Children cried out in alarm and tried to move aside. Plates crashed together. Glasses sent water gushing across the tablecloth. A ceramic tureen exploded; its treacly contents spilled across the table, reminding her of the stain in the basement. Her right hand swatted the food from little Sean's clutches and he burst into tears.

"WE—MUST—FAST!"

With a delightful burst of righteous energy, Mary went about clearing the table of its contents. She swept her arms across food, drink, all tableware. Chairs toppled over. Children ran. Some laughed nervously, some screamed and shouted, many cried. Her left hand felt revelatory with its fireworks display of pain, crashing in chorus with her heart and with her laughter.

Two powerful hands gripped her shoulders and yanked her backward, away from the table. Her back slammed against the hutch, which gave a colossal groan of protest but did not fall. Ines thrust her face—bruised and bloody and livid—into Mary's.

"Stop this, Sister. Stop right now. You've scared the children and wasted our food. What has gotten into you?"

Mary beamed back. "The answer to my prayers, Sister. We must fast! It's the only way to save—"

"Luke died a few hours ago."

Mary froze. Her smile slipped. She blinked at Ines.

"What? N-no . . . no, that can't be true. I refuse to believe. We—we must—"

"Mary. Please." Ines loosened her grip. The eye not swollen shut was red and puffy from crying. "The children need us to be strong."

As the truth sank in, Mary's whole world shrank down to Ines and her pleading face. Her words echoed over and over again—*Luke died a few hours ago . . .*

Luke died a few hours ago . . .

Luke died . . . Luke is dead.

The kitchen door rattled open and shut and Eustace appeared. She wore trousers and gloves awash with dirt, her gray hair wild with sweat, and her face looked as if it had aged a hundred years in the span of a day. She looked at the sisters, seeming not to notice the chaos of the dining table or the cowering children.

"Grave's dug," was all she said before she trudged her way through the mess and disappeared into her office. Her door slammed shut, finally popping Mary's shiny bubble of hope.

XI.

*I*t did not take long for Sister Killjoy to catch
up on the comings and goings of St. Teresa's
residents directly following their benefactor's visit. Mary
woke a few days later to find the window of her room
boarded up with wooden planks nailed over it from the
outside. She didn't bother closing the curtains as she'd
been doing every morning before sunrise; each night,
saying a prayer, she'd placed the crucifix on the moon-
light-bathed windowsill.

That still, small voice had not returned.

She'd never given up trying, though. She wanted to
—*desperately* she wanted to. She wanted to run back
home to her stern, thunderous father, because even stern
and thunderous was preferable to this—this *abandonment*.
But that was silly little Dory talking. Not Sister Mary
Matthew, with her bottomless well of resolve. *Bottomless*
meant never-ending. *Bottomless* meant that her own
private supply of resilience, that reservoir of steadfast
moral fortitude, would go on for eternity. It meant that
no matter how often she needed to draw that strength

from deep within herself, it would never dry up; it would *always be there*.

And so, every second not spent with the children was spent alone on her knees, drawing bucket after bucket from that well again and again. In truth, far more of her time was spent away from the children since baby Luke passed to the other side. Even now, days after her outburst at the dining table, many of the under-fives seemed afraid of her. Which was ludicrous. Simply absurd. Children—afraid of her? How could their fear be so misplaced? Why, *she* was Sister *Funtime*!

But very well. She would win back the joyous hearts of St. Teresa's youth. Just as she would win back that beautiful sleigh-bell laugh from Ines. As she would win back her Savior, and once again she would frolic and sing with the children, smiling from ear to ear, the crucifix a throbbing length of comfort tucked inside her habit. That bottomless well of resolve would fortify her.

To show her confidence in this, she'd unceremoniously tossed out her ratty nightgown and only wore her full nun's regalia. Pieces she'd previously gone without she now borrowed from Ines, her outfit complete and, as far as she was concerned, a permanent fixture of her being: the black wool of the habit skirt draped over her legs, the sleeves of her blouse billowing out, the cape like a lead blanket; the neckerchief and cap were starched to an almost luminescent white, and together with the serretête cinched across her scalp were all held perfectly in place beneath the veil. If she could return the pulsating crucifix to her breast, and perhaps rescue her rosary beads and Bible from Eustace's office, then Sister Mary Matthew would be complete.

"Soon," she promised herself.

Yes, she would charge onward, ever onward. She filled her Savior with moonlight every night and prayed to him all through the day. She'd even stretched up on her toes and snatched the miniature cross from where it hung, the only décor in her room. She'd thought it mahogany, but on inspection it revealed itself to be made of even cheaper stuff than the crucifix that now sat in Eustace's locked desk drawer. The stain it left on the wall suggested it hadn't been touched in years, and she felt a strange sadness for it. It, too, abandoned in this closet of a room. She clutched it as she prayed, worrying at its surface, warming it, until—

Snap!

She gazed, mortified, at the severed left hand of the crossbeam. It had cracked so easily, like the glazed sugar atop the crème brûlée her mother made for Easter Sunday. She tried to fit the broken piece back into place, but it was a clean break. One more tragedy heaped upon the pile, one last straw on the camel's proverbial back. Mary broke, weeping tears she'd thought had all dried up by now. She grew manic, uselessly mashing the broken pieces together, willing them to fit, to mend, to come back together.

"Ah!"

A needle-thin splinter broke from the cross and stabbed itself into the meat of her palm. She quickly tugged it free and held it up for examination: a ruby of her blood beaded from its tip. It shone a pearly black in the darkness. She stared at it, the rest of the world falling away.

She whispered, "Blood sacrifice."

She whispered, "Expiation."

When pressed into the nail bed of her left thumb, the

cross splinter produced a sensation that to Mary felt like rebirth. Like a lightning bolt sent from the heavens to crack her open so that God may examine what lay inside her heart. The tip of the splinter wiggled around in the blood vessels and nerves collecting there. As she applied more pressure, she marveled at the way the thumb branched out in an unnatural direction. The way her fingers had been mangled made her hand look like some kind of scabrous crustacean skittering across the bottom of the ocean. She cried out again—

"*AH!*"

—and pressed harder, until inkblots of viscous light swam and swirled in her vision and bled away her awareness. Her body thumped heavily to the floor.

When she came to—minutes later, hours, days—it felt as if not a single second had passed, like her train of thought still rumbled along the rollercoaster, never derailed from its tracks.

Expiation. Mary's lips curled into a smile. How very Old Testament of her. If Sister Killjoy prescribed to the older scriptures, then Sister Funtime would fall in lockstep and march right along like the good little nun she was.

A knock at the door.

A tremulous voice: "Sister . . . ?"

A vertical blade of light split the gloom as her door creaked open. A face appeared. Déjà vu hit: the bruised and bloody face of Ines, staring out at her. But this face was unharmed, and quite young, barely seventeen years old.

"Lizzie." Mary's voice, husky now, was still a whisper.

"Can I come in?" The girl's eyes were wide.

"Quickly now."

Lizzie slipped inside, the door clicking shut behind her. She uttered a soft sound of alarm, as if just now realizing the only source of light had come from the hall. In the cover of darkness, Mary snatched the crucifix from the cot and shoved it back on the windowsill, tucked out of sight beside the curtains.

"There's a lamp on the dresser."

A few fumbling moments, then a shaded bulb illuminated the room. Mary squinted her eyes against it. She wasn't sure she had the strength to do anything other than stay where she was, kneeling before her cot; she hadn't properly eaten in days.

As Lizzie came to sit near her on the cot, Mary surreptitiously tucked her left hand out of sight beneath her habit sleeve. Her thumb tingled where the splinter still pierced it, but the rest of her hand had turned numb; cold tendrils of paresthesia writhed along her upper arm. She gave the girl her right hand and squeezed, offering her what she hoped was some semblance of a comforting smile.

"What is it I can do for you, child?"

Lizzie returned the smile, but only just. It was then that Mary noticed the girl's haunted expression. This was exacerbated by hollow cheeks and a painfully prominent collarbone. Her brown hair lay in greasy clumps.

"Perhaps you can forgive me for calling you a child," Mary added, nudging the girl's knee. It was true that she was approaching skin-and-bones, yet still her womanhood shone through. In a flash, she reminded Mary of herself: it had only been a few years since *she'd* been that age, after all. "Please. You can speak plainly."

Lizzie's ghost of a smile grew a little more; she

brushed away a tear before it could fall. "Sister, we're . . ." She cleared her throat. "We're worried about you."

Mary's mind nearly broke from the dissonance: children—the very children to whom she'd sworn her love and protection—worried about *her*. It should be the other way around. This was wrong—

"You haven't left your room," the girl went on. "Have you eaten? Can I . . . bring you something?"

Lizzie's face swam in her vision. Tears broke the light into fractals.

"You know," Mary said, looking away to hide her face, "I remember the taxicab ride here, for my first day at St. Teresa's. The road kept climbing, up, up, up the mountain . . . so many trees, such a clear sky, every city left far behind. It felt"—she smiled, tears salting her lips—"like I was ascending to heaven." She glanced shyly at Lizzie. "That's how I thought of it. Leaving my life on this earth to ascend to a higher form of existence. I loved the name I'd picked out. Sister Mary Matthew. But . . . truth be told, I loved my old name, too." She whispered it, sharing a secret glimpse into the hidden compartments of her soul: *"Dorothea* . . . fun, silly little Dory." She chuckled, a gurgle in her throat. "Between you and me, Lizzie, I think I've committed a terrible sin in lying to myself. I lied about who I was, or maybe about who I wanted to be. I think a part of me knew, and so hid away those parts of me—those *Dory* parts—somewhere deep inside. Like at the bottom of a well." She lifted up on her knees so that she was nearly at eye level with Lizzie and gazed steadily at her. "Promise me—promise yourself—that you'll never do that. That you'll never hide who you are."

Lizzie smirked. "Who I am? The girl nobody wanted, who sneaks around an orphanage full of little kids?"

"*Yes*. Don't you see? Be that girl. Be who you are no matter what life you've been dealt. So yes, sneak around the orphanage, steal communion wine, kiss the cute boy—"

Lizzie giggled, looked at the door as if Killjoy might appear.

"—and keep your name. *Lizzie*. It's a beautiful name."

Lizzie squeezed her hand, and a serious expression settled on her face. "Sister, you didn't just lose Dory. She's still in here." She reached tentatively out and rested one hand against Mary's habit, where once the crucifix pulsed. It sent a jolt through her. "I mean, think about it. Where do you think Sister Funtime came from?"

The girl lunged clumsily forward, eager in her embarrassment, and hugged Mary tightly. Before anything further could be said, she stood and flitted to the door. Before she was gone, she turned at the threshold, looking back.

"And please . . . forgive yourself for Luke. It's not your fault."

Mary wanted desperately for this to be true, and so did not trust herself to respond. Instead, she smiled warmly back.

"Besides," Lizzie added, "if he had gotten better, and grown up, and had to meet Mr. James . . ." She shuddered. "It's better this way."

And she was gone.

Every warm and fuzzy feeling evaporated, and filling Mary up in a torrent of bubbling sludge was that familiar feeling of dread. She bolted up, sending stars wheeling in her vision. She tasted bile.

"Wait! Lizzie!"

She tore across the room, catching the girl only a few steps down the hall. She looked frightened, as if Mary had caught her already breaking her promise.

"What does that mean?" Mary said, her voice choked with fear. "What . . . how could you say that, 'it's better this way'? What do you mean, he'd have to meet Mr. James?"

"I . . . I thought you knew." Lizzie stepped closer, not speaking above a whisper. "Mr. James, he—" Her face flushed; tears poured. "He—*likes*—children. He fucking *loves* them. And if he takes a special liking to one of us, one of his little orphans, he'll take us on a 'field trip,' just one on one. Usually, we'll never see them again."

Mary's face was slack with horror. "Usually?"

"Well . . ." Lizzie gulped. "If they come back, Killjoy gets her shovel."

Mary's vision, still dancing with stars, flashed with images:

Ines, her face beaten to a pulp.

The cemetery, with its barely marked graves.

EZEKIEL 1920 . . . ISAAC 1918 . . . MILLIE & DEBORAH 1899 . . . PETER R.I.P. . . . RUTH 19—.

That single word etched in the stone: BABY.

Little Thomas, hiding and afraid to see Mr. James.

And, finally, Sister Agatha Eustace, standing in dirt-covered trousers.

Grave's dug.

"No," Mary breathed. "No, it can't be. I refuse—"

When her vision finally settled, there was Lizzie still in the hall. Her wide eyes shimmered with hurt. "I thought you knew," she said, and then ran off.

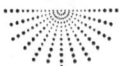

XII

*M*ary spilled back into her room, leaving the door thrown wide.

Lizzie's parting words rang in her head like an apocalyptic belfry.

I thought you knew.

I thought you knew.

I thought you knew.

She stumbled, slamming her shoulder into the windowsill and awakening that old ache. The crucifix spun away, knocked to the floor, where it skidded to a halt within the glowing oval of lamplight. It lay face down, the miniature cross pressing the spreadeagled body of Christ into the sagging and worn floorboards.

Mary held her breath, staring. The crucifix didn't move. He didn't speak. She stayed her reflex to immediately right it. Instead, she slowly pushed herself toward it with her right arm, favoring her left hand and shoulder.

When she finally reached the crucifix, she bent over it, the tip of her nose just inches away from the cross's wooden backing. A tear spilled down her nose and splashed upon it. Her breath finally released with the whisper:

"Why didn't you tell me?"

She dropped fully and rolled to her back beside the crucifix, staring up at the ceiling and letting her tears shed.

"St. Teresa's is not a place of God," she said. "It is evil. It is run by a vile, sinful man who commits vile sins against its children. Why would God allow such a place to shroud itself in his guise, let alone exist? I know there is evil in the world—I *know* this—but . . . what is the point of fighting it if it can hide itself in your light and— and—" Speech became a struggle; panic bubbled up her throat, choking her. "—and I dedicated my *life* to this place. I lent a hand to the devil and thought him God, I . . . the pain and suffering and blood of children stains my hands and I did not see. Even with Christ himself by my side." She turned her head, peering again at the still crucifix. "Why didn't you tell me? Why didn't you *warn* me?"

Silence.

She raised herself on one arm and screamed:

"TELL ME!"

Still, silence.

She scoffed bitterly. "You are no savior. You are not Jesus Christ of Nazareth. You, like this place, are the devil in disguise."

Even before the words had fully left her, she felt an invisible force, like a gust of wind, sweep her into the dresser.

CRASH!

She cried out amid splintering wood. She'd never filled the dresser's drawers, so there was no clothing to pad her body. The dresser toppled over her and fell heavily to the side, sending the lamp spinning to one corner. Its shade skittered away as the trailing cord jerked it back, and the bulb smashed against the ground in a shower of glass. The bulb's filament, like a miniature coil of lightning, fizzed out as it oxidized and burned away, sending traces of mercury into the air.

She was aware dimly of other shouts of alarm somewhere in the mansion, but they were quickly drowned out by his voice, no longer small but like a howling gale.

YOU DARE QUESTION ME, DORY?!

Mary's temple throbbed. She picked herself up from the splintered wreckage, crawled to him.

"Master . . . please . . ."

Let me look upon you.

Carefully, reverently, she plucked the crucifix from the floor and placed it so that his sapphire eyes shone up at her.

Good girl, he said.

The sight of her left hand beside him, fingers mangled beyond use, caught her eye, and she winced. She'd tried to ignore the festering wounds, tried to tell herself that the pain was *good*, the pain was her willing sacrifice. But now she could not look away. Now she saw. The flesh was swollen, looked shiny and raw, as if badly sunburned. The places where bone had pushed through the skin had turned infectious, mottled in frightening shades of olive and umber between bloody scabs. Pockets of bruised yellow bulged from her knuckles, pearlescent lakes of pus just waiting to burst.

Look at me.

She did.

Do not mistake your inability to understand my plan for

anything other than exactly that. *Dory, Dory, Dory . . . forever foolish, forever stupid. When will you trust in your Master?*

She shook with sobs. "Master . . . forgive me . . ."

Do not presume I knew nothing of the comings and goings of this place. Why do you think I appeared to you in the first place? I needed you, Dory. I needed—still need—Sister Mary Matthew as my agent on the inside. Hast thou forsaken me?

She tucked away the gruesome sight of her hand. The memory of its breaking flashed through her mind: the window slicing down on it with a *crack!* All because her Lord had led her to believe that she should have brought Thomas to Mr. James right away. But if she had . . . with everything she now knew of this place and its mysterious owner . . . wouldn't she have been consigning a child to death, even perhaps to something far worse?

"Never, my Lord," she whispered. Her voice had turned flat, dead of emotion. Desperately she tried to clear the doubts still swirling like a storm cloud just behind her eyes. Shame withered her heart.

Yes. Well.

Her Christ's use of Eustace's pet phrase snagged in her mind, almost made her gasp.

You'll be needing a new necklace.

She nodded, grasping his meaning. In quick, unhesitating movements, she coiled another thick braid of hair from beneath the cloth of her serre-tête and yanked it free of its roots. He whispered to her as she returned his crucifix to its rightful place over her heart.

Good. Now. I have yet to fully forgive you for your betrayals, but your sacrifice shall slowly but surely rebalance the scales of your soul.

She smiled, finally feeling that happy rush of uncomplicated devotion. She was Jonah, and St. Teresa's was her whale. Her breath expelled with the single word, "Expiation."

Yes. Good. Tell me, Sister Mary Matthew, who in this house would stand to benefit from Mr. James's arrangement?

Mary thought of that locked cash box, bursting but hidden away.

"Sister Killjoy."

Perhaps it is time we pay her a visit.

Her smile widened. "Yes."

She lifted herself and made for the door.

Wait.

She halted. "Yes?"

The time for concealment is over, he said. *The truth of St. Teresa's has revealed itself to you, and so we must do the same. Wear me with pride, Dory.*

Her jaw gave an audible crack as her smile widened still further. Fumbling in her excitement and giggling, as if undressing on her wedding night, Mary pulled the crucifix from beneath her habit and restrung it so that it lay in the open, her Master dangling from her chest for all to see. His arms spread wide as if in welcome, sapphire eyes glinting above his own smile.

THE DOOR GAVE beneath her aching shoulder, but there was no Sister Agatha Eustace on the other side. Mary checked for a hidden compartment, a closet, *anything*, but the office was empty. She stopped, breathing in time with the crucifix as it pulsated against the fabric of her habit.

"Where could she be?"

But he didn't say.

Her eyes rested on the Virgin Mary figurine, still perfectly centered on Eustace's immaculate desktop. It stared at her with a wholly unattached expression. Mary suddenly hated its affected reverence, its condescension. But worst of all, she hated how smugly it hid Eustace's key to her treasure. It guarded the key to Mary's own personal belongings—everything she had in the world. And, worst of all, that pilfered cash box, hidden away from doing any good in the world, in an orphanage of all places. *Blood* money was what it was, and the Virgin Mary was sullied.

Mary screamed her frustration, picked up the figurine, and smashed it against the wall. Ceramic slivers showered her in a white dust that settled over the black of her habit like a shroud. Still, she screamed, her voice inarticulate as it tore through the air.

A tinny *ping* announced the hidden key, now at her feet.

She stared at it, breathing heavily. "She's not here."

No.

"Then why am I?"

Do not underestimate the importance of righteous anger, Dory. You will need it for what I would have you do.

Her head spun. Vertigo slammed into her like God's fist. The only thing keeping her on her feet was the anchoring weight of her fury.

"I am ready," she said. "I will do it. Whatever you ask. Please."

You are not ready, he said. *But . . . almost.*

She ached to prove herself to him, to show him that she was ready and willing to put an end to the evil taking place at St. Teresa's. Gone were her hesitations. Her hands were steadier than ever, even the left, its pains shunted from her perception. She did as he instructed, swiping the key from the floor and unlocking the drawer.

When she turned to leave the office, cash box and alcohol bottle clutched to her habit, she nearly ran into Ines.

The sister stood just past the threshold of the office, gazing at her in alarm. She wore a silk nightgown, and her hair was unbound and uncovered, a shiny black river cascading down her back. The bruises and swelling still on her face bolstered Mary's righteous anger—that James! To have hurt her Ines like this? She could strangle him.

The thought, the savagery of it, gave her brief pause; but then the crucifix throbbed hotly through her clothing and she reveled in the heat of it. She brushed past Ines, who stepped haltingly after her.

"Mary . . . the children, they're frightened. We heard your shouts, and just now screaming. Are . . . are you okay?"

Something Ines once said to her echoed in her mind —*I'll hear everything you do and say. Beware!*—and suddenly Mary's heart ached for that first day at St. Teresa's, when she'd first met Sister Ines Joseph. In truth, on that day so long ago she'd fallen in love with Ines. Or maybe a schoolgirl's crush. A fact which no longer filled her with a secret shame. But the memory, and seeing how much they'd both changed, nearly broke her heart.

Oh, silly little Dory, he whispered.

Mary whirled around. She thrust the cash box into the sister's arms. "Take it. It's not Eustace's to hide away." She turned to leave, considered, and added, "Round up the children. Pack whatever they need. You'll —" Her voice faltered, and she was suddenly glad she was not looking Ines in the eye. "You'll want to leave this place. All of you. Please."

"What—"

"As soon as you can. *Please*, Ines. The children are in danger. And I think you already know that in your heart. Get as far away from here as you can. As soon as you can. This very night."

She strode to the kitchen, shutting away Ines's protesting voice. She rummaged beneath the sink and came back up now clutching, alongside the liquor bottle, the bleach, vinegar, and lye. She was happy to see that Ines was not there when she turned back, but she knew she couldn't return to her own room. She might lack the strength for the next part.

It would have to be the basement.

She thought of her pocket-size Bible, still in Eustace's unlocked drawer beside her rosary beads and old crucifix. The Bible was full of signs, full of grand gestures to prove one's devotion to God. Especially the Old Testament. Jonah repented while in the belly of the whale. And if St. Teresa's had a belly, it was the basement.

She was surprised to see a slice of moonlight on the basement floor. When had nighttime arrived? She did not know. Time itself had left her; it was elusive, illusory, a great trench of nothingness into which she'd obediently plunged, fully faithful that her Lord would bear her out on angel's wings.

As her eyes adjusted to the gloom, a shape etched itself into her vision, like an artist's charcoal rubbing. The sight of it sent a shock through her and she dropped the bundle in her arms to the dirt floor.

It was a baby's crib. Luke's bed. Someone had deposited it here after his death.

Grave's dug.

Eustace's words fueled her rage further. Her vision

blotted out the crib. She dropped to her knees in that slice of moonlight and collected the dropped items, lining them up for their intended purpose.

Expiation.

"Master," she whispered. The crucifix gave a pulse of heat in response. It hissed against the fabric. "I am yours. I am your agent, in the belly of the beast. I am your vessel, and you my compass. With these I cleanse my soul so that I might do your bidding as a heated blade cuts butter. This is my expiation. My penance. For you."

The litany continued from her lips with every breath. As she prayed, she picked up the bleach—a large brown glass bottle, its green label partially rubbed off so that all that was legible was CLOROX WILL BE YOUR WILLING SERVANT! She'd rolled away her left sleeve, and now she poured the strong-smelling liquid over her injured hand. It hissed on contact. There was a brief pause in her prayer, but she did not scream. She watched, transfixed, as the gangrenous skin boiled and popped; viscous pus bubbled and trickled to the dirt. One knuckle bone shone brightly through, as clean as virgin snow.

After applying it to her right hand and forearms as well, she set down the bleach. Next, the vinegar: the cork popped from the small glass bottle and she poured the clear liquid over each hand, rubbing them together and massaging it into every crease of her skin. An overpowering smell raised from her hands like a fine mist, and she breathed it in like incense. A red liquid seeped from her skin and slicked over her hands: blood.

"For you," she breathed, smiling at the pain. Its burn was transcendent.

More, he said. The fabric his crucifix touched briefly caught fire and smoldered to ash.

Her ablutions performed, the skin of both hands and forearms purified, she turned next to the lye. The boxy tin can was nearly empty, but the layer of powder at the bottom would be enough. Her mouth watered at the sight of it, salivating, collecting pools of spit beneath her tongue. She poured the lye into her mouth like sugar. As it and her saliva were swallowed down, they became like liquid fire. A rope of flame, from her tonsils to her chest, etched every inch of her throat in bubbling, cleansing heat. She guzzled it down, craning her head back and staring at the low ceiling. Every sensation in her body — her stinging hands, her bruised knees pressing into the unforgiving dirt — fell away, leaving only her fiery throat. Never again would that horrible sensation from before, that strangling, turgid darkness, that bubbling sludge of dread, clog her throat. She would be pure. She would be born again in the fires of her devotion.

Yes, he said. *Good.*

She grinned, head still craned back, and she laughed, a hacking, coughing engine of a laugh. Dark spots of glistening blood sprayed the ceiling, gleaming in the dark like individual rubies. She laughed, and the moon sang to her, and he burned into her heart.

"Sister. What in hell's name are you doing?"

Sister Agatha Eustace stood just feet away, a lit lantern in one hand. She wore a plain, voluminous night-gown, her hair in a tight bun, and she stood with her back facing the far reaches of the basement, as if she had just come from there rather than from the stairs. Mary was suddenly sure that she'd finally discovered the older sister's sleeping quarters. That slumbering creature,

Sister Killjoy this entire time? The irony was not lost on Mary.

"It is after hours, Sister," Eustace went on. "You should be sleeping. For God's sake, what do you plan to do with all that nonsense"—she gestured at the chemicals lined up before Mary—"clean the *dirt*? I imagine all you'll find beneath it is more dirt, you stupid girl."

Just days before, such words would have deeply affected Mary. But that part of her—that *Dory* part—was finally gone. Scrubbed away with bleach and vinegar and lye and the power of Sister Mary Matthew's devotion to her Savior.

Mary stood, calm and steady, and faced Eustace.

"You have much to confess, Sister," Mary said.

Eustace scoffed, throwing up a hand in exasperation and looking around as if to show everyone how delusional this girl was. But there was no one. When Mary did not blink, did not look away, Eustace finally spoke. "What, for the baby? You think his death my fault? I told you then and I'll tell you now, you brat, that child's fate was entirely up to God. No doctor—no medicine—no amount of prayers or fasts could change . . . What are you doing—"

As the sister spoke, Mary had walked slowly toward her, closer and closer with every word, until finally, having heard enough, she whipped out her hand and slapped Eustace hard across the face.

"You *bitch*!" Eustace gasped, one hand cradling her cheek. She pulled her fingers away, looking at the strange liquid substance that had splashed from Mary's hand. "What—what is this—"

"Confess," Mary repeated.

Eustace stood there, her face livid, mouth open but

silent, red blooming on her cheek even in the low light. Finally, she stuttered, "It's just occurred to me . . . I believe the last time I caught you sneaking into the basement I threatened dire consequences. Well, you'll find that I am no liar. First thing tomorrow you're out on your ass, and I'll personally see that you'll never wear that habit again."

Mary smiled. "Oh, Sister, we both know you are very much a liar."

"Whatever are you on about now?"

Say it, he whispered.

"Mr. James?" Mary said. "You've looked the other way all these years, letting that man do what he does. What was it that you said to me? 'It is not our job to protect the children'? Neither is it your job to hide away the Order's money in that cash box. Neither is it to bury discarded children in your backyard and hide away proof of their existence down here."

Eustace's eyes darted to the crates full of papers behind Mary for a brief moment. Then, surprise of all surprises, she looked into Mary's eyes and she grinned and she laughed. It was a hideous sound, and the smile on her face only served to make her look as hideous on the outside as she was on the inside, the witch-like visage of an old crone. The lantern swung from her convulsions, throwing shadow puppets spinning along the walls.

"My, look at this," Eustace said, stepping toward her. "The stupid little girl from Syracuse has been sneaking around where she doesn't belong. And what? You think you can shame me, make me run to the nearest old pervert's confessional? My girl, your naïveté is tragic."

Eustace moved to the side, stepping in a wide arc around Mary as she spoke.

"You think that stupid Mr. James is my *master*? You think I'd kowtow to any man? *Wake* up!" Her voice had climbed to a chalkboard screech, shocking Mary from the white-hot center of her righteous anger. "The only thing they teach you in that little Bible of yours is that women are second-rate. Eve from Adam's rib, Lot's nameless wife turned to salt, weary-eyed Leah consoled with the gift of several bratty children—*pah!*"

As Eustace spoke, circling her, Mary pivoted where she stood.

"Welcome to the *new* order, Sister," the old woman continued. "I serve a *new* master now, one with powers that old has-been in the sky hasn't shown us since the days of the Old Testament. That idiot Mr. James is just a means to an end, a golden goose whose eggs will pay for the construction of something far greater than St. Teresa's Joyous Youths Orphanage."

She'd reached the stairs, one foot creaking onto the first step. Eustace grinned malevolently down at Mary and spat out:

"It's a shame you'll not live to see it!"

And she turned her back on Mary and tromped heavily up the stairs.

Stop her, he whispered. *She'll lock you down here!*

When she did not move—shocked into paralysis by the sheer blasphemy of Eustace's words—the crucifix glowed like a stoked fire, sizzling through her habit entirely and pressing into her chest with a *hssssss!*

Mary yelled out, galvanized into action. She leapt forward, springing up the steps, and managed to claw the hem of Eustace's nightgown. The old woman screeched and tried to pull away, but Mary gave a mighty tug—

"*AIIIIIIIIIII!*"

—and brought the woman crashing down the stairs. She collided into Mary, knocked her down, and continued her fall, sprawling past the window and into the far wall. With a crash, the discarded baby's crib finally broke her fall. She lay, moaning, in a mess of splintered furniture.

In the ensuing silence, Mary climbed to her feet. The crucifix did not swing from the braid around her neck: it had embedded itself into the flesh between her breasts. She braced herself, catching her breath, but the older woman did not stir. Sister Eustace was out cold.

Quickly now, he said.

"What would you have me do?" Mary whispered.

Give Killjoy the same fate she failed to give you.

She paused. Frowned. Her Savior would have her leave the woman to her death? Something about this felt . . . wrong. But then the crucifix throbbed a deep red. Her mind swept itself of any doubt, focusing on that pulse just over her own heart.

She smiled. "Yes," she breathed.

She could hear the smile in his voice when he answered her, *You are finally ready.*

Her smile grew. She scooped the liquor bottle from the dusty floor and turned toward the stairs. But before she climbed them, something familiar reached her ears. She paused just long enough to hear the heavy, ragged breathing of some monstrous creature deep in the depths of the basement.

"Huh," she muttered. "It wasn't Eustace after all."

Hurry now. We're running out of moonlight.

"Yes, Master."

At the top of the stairs, Mary slammed the basement door behind her.

XIII

"Quickly, children, quickly now! Tabitha, take Lizzie's hand. Benjamin, grab a couple blankets for the littles, it'll be freezing out there!"

St. Teresa's had come to life. Kids were shouting across the upstairs wards, hurrying excitedly this way and that, moth-eaten coats thrown over their hand-me-down pajamas. Someone had turned on all the lights, including the chandelier, below which stood Ines.

"Five more minutes! Hurry your butts down here!"

In the commotion, it seemed that no one had noticed the shouts and crashing sounds from the basement. Mary emerged into a beehive of activity. She reached Ines as the last of the children thundered down the stairs and out the front door, which stood wide open to the night. Cold air rushed inside, making the chandelier swing drunkenly where it hung.

When Ines saw her, she didn't return Mary's smile. Instead, she clapped both hands over her open mouth, her chocolate eyes wide. She lowered her hands and reached hesitantly for Mary.

"Sister . . . what happened to you? You're—you're bleeding!"

She swept a finger down Mary's chin, coming away with syrupy blood.

Mary turned to the foyer mirror. Her jaw and neck were slathered in a thick stream of blood so dark in color it was almost black. She smiled at herself, her white teeth gleaming.

Ines pulled Mary's face from the mirror, gently cradled in her soft hands, and looked into her eyes. "Sister, I don't know what it is that is happening. But I trust in you. So I am doing as you said. I'm taking the children and the cash box and we are getting far away from this place. But, Mary, please . . . *come with us.*"

Mary smiled benevolently back at her. "Oh, my Ines . . ." She dipped her head forward, out of Ines's grasp, and kissed her cheek. As her bottom lip was tacky with blood, it left a half kiss imprinted among the bruises collected there. "I love you. I am so glad to have known you. But I still have work to do here."

A tear splashed down the other sister's cheek. "I'll send a taxi back for you, then."

"No need," Mary replied, winking. "I've the bicycle."

Ines nodded, not responding. But the truth was there in her big eyes: she knew Mary would not be leaving St. Teresa's. Whether she remembered that Eustace had confiscated the bicycle's tire, or because, somehow, she understood that this was a mission her sister was determined to face alone.

"Adiós," Ines whispered, and she turned and left.

Mary felt a distant pang in her heart. She wished dearly that she could hear that sleigh-bell laughter one last time. But it was not to be. Not in this life. Still, as

Ines approached the fountain where all the children had congregated, Mary called out one final goodbye:

"Small rebellions, Sister!"

As she turned to her next task, she heard Ines faintly call back:

"They're good for the heart."

HE HAD GIVEN Mary her final instructions.

St. Teresa's Joyous Youths Orphanage was to be razed to the earth.

She began with the chapel. The sacrilege of such an act felt almost sensual, a secret rebellion for the sake of her Master. Retrieving the liquor bottle and a handful of matches from the kitchen, she slipped out the back door and fought the icy wind along the path leading to the chapel. Inside, she danced and sang as she lit dozens of prayer candles, spilling the alcohol across the pews as she went.

"Welcome, welcome, welcome . . ."

With the moon out and shining through the stained glass window, the sense of déjà vu skittered up her spine, and she was teleported briefly back to the night she snuck into the cemetery, lighting matches between rows of headstones not unlike these rows of pews. It gave her a thrill, and she stole into the back room to retrieve some communion wine to whet her throat, which was scorched.

At last, back at the double oak doors of the entrance, she spilled a dripping candle to the floor, and its flame snaked through the room. In seconds the place was alive with crackling light. She watched as it climbed the large statue of Jesus upon his cross, then continued on her way.

The schoolhouse went up with the help of some generator gasoline she found in the shed next to the greenhouse. She scrawled on the blackboard as the flames grew around her, WELCOME TO HELL, then danced back outside, her voice climbing an octave.

"Come on inside, smile wide . . ."

The mansion was ultimately a much larger task. She flicked the gas on, the air over the stove shimmering like a living thing; she drenched the curtains in reeking ethanol. She coaxed the flames with the children's bedsheets. When she could no longer stand the smoke, she skipped down the front steps. She'd stuffed a rag down the neck of the liquor bottle, which she now tossed with all her strength. It smashed through a windowpane, feeding the hungry fire with a fresh supply of cold night air oxygen.

She stood now on the stone lip of the fountain, facing the burning furnace that once was St. Teresa's, and the light of the flames reflected in her wide, gleeful eyes. The moon hid itself behind thick columns of smoke pouring toward the heavens. The heat rose like a physical wall before her, singeing her eyebrows, yet still it did not approach the intensity of the crucifix, still pulsating at the center of her being. Surely the children were long gone now, trekking down the winding gravel road with Ines, but one last spark of that old Dory imagination sent a distant chanting sound to her ears:

"Sister Funtime! Sister Funtime! Sister Funtime!"

She beamed, rapturous. The children were giving her a farewell. She could even pluck out the perfectly in-sync voices of her favorites, those two little angels, Hanna and Haley.

As if to add percussion to the chorus, thunder boomed somewhere in the vast night sky. Forks of lightning flicked in the distance. A rain burst from above, briefly clearing the smoke from covering the moon. But she did not fear the rain. The inferno was a living thing now, its rage too fierce to be put out by a little storm. She laughed and beamed up at it as raindrops sizzled against her feverish skin.

You have one final task, he said, breaking her spell.

"Yes, Master!" she sang.

He told her where to go.

AROUND THE SIDE of the burning mansion, cleverly hidden behind a façade of vines and boughs, was a red cellar door. Its padlock may as well have been a disguise, for at her touch it simply melted away. The doors swung easily apart, and she climbed down a steep, crumbling staircase of stone.

"Eustace's own private basement entrance," she said.

Yes.

At the bottom she found herself at the mouth of a tunnel. It looked to be hewn crudely from the earth, and seemed to wind down, deep underground. From it came that same ragged, sonorous breathing of some unknown creature. Eustace's master. Its breathing was much louder here, and Mary briefly wondered just how big it must be, or even what it was. She was not sure she wanted to venture closer to find out.

Stand back, he instructed.

She backed away from the winding tunnel, waited.

"Master, what — ?"

Quiet. I must concentrate.

She held her breath. Waited.

Several long seconds later, there came a rumbling from the tunnel walls. It grew and grew, and she began to feel as if she were in the midst of an earthquake. Dust sifted down. Mary coughed and backed away. In the commotion she could not find the steps to the cellar door, stumbling farther along until she was in the basement proper. Finally, with a deafening roar, an impenetrable wall of rock caved in the tunnel entrance.

It is done.

She felt she mustn't ask what *it* was.

The rumbling slowly died away, so that she could hear the raging inferno above. The ceiling groaned as its integrity ebbed away.

"YOU THINK YOU'VE WON?!"

Before she could react to the voice, a body slammed into Mary's back. She fell to the dirt, squirming around to face the crazed woman atop her. Eustace's face glared dementedly down at her, the bun of hair spilled apart in wild zigzags of gray. Her withered old hands found Mary's throat beneath her neckerchief and clawed the breath from her.

"Youuuuuu little *bitch*," Eustace seethed. Fetid breath spilled like death over Mary's face, hissing past the older woman's cracked, brown teeth. "You think any of what you've done matters? You think you're acting on behalf of *God*?! Foolish little girl. You think you see the truth, but you are *blind*!"

Her eyes darkled with evil intent. She raised her hands from Mary's windpipe, crawling up her face as life-giving air whistled back down her throat. Eustace's thumbs reached Mary's eyes. She jabbed at Mary and leaned forward, grinning like a loon.

"*Blind* is what you are, Sister *Funtime*."

Mary screamed as the old woman's bony thumbs pressed themselves deep into her eye sockets. Bright pain anchored her into place, and she screamed and screamed but could not move as Eustace pushed harder, digging her thumbs deeper. Finally, the pressure released in a horrifying rupture. Her vision burst into a dazzling black. Runny, gelatinous wet seeped down her face.

Suddenly, Eustace was gone, thrown from her body, perhaps from whatever force the crucifix still possessed after causing the cave-in. Mary scrambled up into a sitting position, staring blindly around but seeing nothing.

Her chest burned as if skewered with a poker, and her screams turned to yells of ecstasy. The crucifix sizzled and spat with heat. The pain from her burst eyeballs grew distant, drowned in this new sensation. Her entire world shrank to a single shape at the center of her body: the cross, burning itself through her chest and to her heart.

She scrambled to her feet. The world glowed around her, the cross's heat radiating outward in waves of supernatural perception. She was not *blind*. Sister Funtime was never blind when following her Master!

She stepped toward Eustace, who backed away, cowering.

"What . . . wait . . . how — ?"

Sister Funtime slammed her hands together, feeling Killjoy's throat between them. She lifted the old woman off her feet, giddy with a strength she'd never known.

When she spoke, she spoke in dual tones: that of Mary Matthew, laced with the whispering voice of her Master.

" *'I will remove the heart of stone from their flesh and give them a heart of flesh.' Do you know what scripture I quote, Sister?*"

Killjoy choked out a garbled response.

"It is from the Book of Ezekiel," Sister Funtime said. *"As you once told me, death is still an answer, is it not?"*

A keening moan issued from Killjoy's throat. Her body squirmed in its final throes, but Mary did not relent her grasp.

"An eye . . . for an eye."

CRACK!

Sister Killjoy became silent as her spine and throat were crushed in Sister Funtime's grasp, sluicing together with an almighty *squelch*. Her hands met, the bone and muscle and skin pulverized to a pulpy mess. The head and body separated, falling away in the grime and dirt of the basement floor. The head bounced away, its eyes staring but seeing nothing, nothing.

Very good, Sister.

Somewhere, the lantern was knocked over. It shattered, lighting the wooden planks of the staircase aflame.

In her new blind world of miasmic heatwaves of vision, Sister Funtime stepped past the discarded corpse to the window. No longer did the moonlight penetrate from above, but she could feel that dark stain climbing the basement wall. It spread out beneath her and pulsated in perfect time with her crucifix, as if one and the same. In its spreading circumference were the shattered remains of Luke's crib.

She dropped to her knees. Felt the crib with seeking hands.

"I am sorry I could not save you, Luke," she whispered, tears washing the eye jelly from her cheeks. "I should have done more. But I saved your brothers and sisters. They are with Ines now. They will never be harmed by this place again."

Her fingers felt for the nails that once pieced together the crib, now sticking out from its broken pieces. With her Master as her guide, she pried them from the wood, collecting the nails in her teeth as she worked.

Your ultimate sacrifice, he whispered to her. *For me.*

Sister Funtime did not respond, for it was not for him that she did this. She did this for Mary. For Mary, she tugged the white cloth of her serre-tête down so that it draped over her unseeing sockets like a shroud. For Mary, she raised the first nail and pressed its tip into her scalp, at her temple, where she had sacrificed her braid for his necklace. Each nail in turn, pressed to her head, embedded in her flesh like thorns. Again and again, spaced at equidistant intervals across the entirety of her scalp, piercing her veil and then the skin and then cracking the glaze of her skull. Like the crème brûlée Mary's mother made for Easter. One by one, for Mary, Sister Funtime built herself a crown of nails.

As she completed her task, the ceiling caved. Fire rained down on her, Sister Funtime's final baptism. She clasped her hands together in prayer and smiled.

Yes! he sang.

She did not reply. Though, secretly, a part of her knew this entity upon her breast was not Jesus, had never in fact been Jesus, he still had been her Savior in his way. And that was enough for Sister Funtime.

After all, with his guidance she had protected the children.

Wreaths of flame engulfed her. That dark stain in the earth crumbled away beneath her knees. Sister Funtime lifted her head and thought of singing children and cotton candy and carnival rides. *That* would be the heaven of her dreams.

SMILEYLAND, 1988.

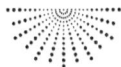

"That was the end of St. Teresa's, but eventually, someone got ahold of the land and rebuilt. Smileyland was born from the ashes. Some say Sister Funtime died that day, that the nails were taken from her head and hammered into this very rollercoaster."

Jess had led the group in a wide circle all around the deserted park as she told her story. Now, as they reached her tale's end, they gazed up at the massive crisscrossing structure of the rollercoaster. Cam shivered for the umpteenth time. Amy, still clutching his arm, felt it and smiled. But she didn't laugh. None of them had laughed, not for a while. Even Brad.

"Okay, fine," Brad admitted, snatching the flashlight back from Jess. "I'll admit your story's maybe a *little* better than mine. But that's just because I was only getting started. I'll tell the *full* tale of Mister Smiley next, and it'll have you shitting your pants and running for Mommy."

Amy gagged. "Gross, dude."

"Cam?" Jess said. "You're awful quiet. What'd you think of my story? Anything as scary as Sister Funtime where you're from?"

Cam frowned. He'd always be the British outsider with the funny accent. He thought maybe that would change if he came along on this trip, but now he wished he'd never stepped foot in Smileyland.

"I don't know about scary," he said.

The others laughed.

He looked around. "What?"

"Boy, you were shivering in your boots that whole time," Amy said.

He shrugged. "It's cold, that's all. Really, if any of that story was true, I feel *bad* for her more than anything. And for those kids."

Brad jumped in front of him, forcing the group to stop in their stroll along the cobblestones. "Come on, dude. You're trying to tell us that if Sister Funtime showed up right now, right here, you wouldn't be scared shitless?"

"Enough with the gross, Brad," Amy groaned.

"Seriously, you wouldn't go running at the first sight of a nun right now? You'd, what, go up to her and pat her on the back because you feel *sorry* for Sister Funtime?"

"Shut up," Cam muttered.

The others kept chatting, but Cam was feeling it even less now. He wanted nothing more than to go home. Besides, it was getting late, wasn't it? He looked up. The moon had climbed across the night sky as Jess told her story, and now it illuminated the side of the rollercoaster facing them.

It really was a cool construction. He'd never been

one for amusement rides, and just looking at that steep dive down the tracks sent butterflies fluttering in his stomach.

"Cam, you coming?"

It was Amy, beckoning for him to keep up with them.

Suddenly, the wind howled. They all gave a collective shiver.

"Yeah, I think it's getting ready to storm," Jess said. "We might wanna hurry back."

A great thunderclap startled them. Lightning forked from the black sky, striking the rollercoaster with a mighty *ZZZZT*. Jess screamed.

"Come on!" Brad yelled.

Cam leapt to catch up with them, and the others turned back to the trail —

They stopped, speechless. The path was blocked. A second ago there wasn't another soul in sight, but now a black figure stood in the middle of the cobblestone path, deathly still and pooled in shadows.

"Hey, sorry!" Brad called out to the figure. "We didn't know there was security here, we're — we're just leaving."

The figure did not respond. Just stood there.

Brad swung the beam of his flashlight over to the figure, and it illuminated a woman dressed in black, swishing skirts, white framing her face. A nun.

Cam's heart stopped.

Her skin was withered and mottled a sickening green, clinging to her skeleton as if shrink-wrapped. A white cloth was draped over her eyes, and sticking all across her scalp, like a bed of needles, were the blackened, burnt fragments of metal nails.

She spoke.

SPENCER HAMILTON

"Welcome to Smileyland, children. Did we remember our prayers?"

They all screamed, and she swept forward, smiling.

AFTERWORD

ON BEGINNINGS: A SMILEYLAND RETROSPECTIVE

To paraphrase previous sentiments (specifically my introduction to my short story collection, *Kitchen Sink*):

Stories are monsters.

To continue that metaphor, some monsters are bigger than others. Some, as Mary Shelley's Viktor Frankenstein eventually learns, have a mind of their own.

Enter Smileyland.

Halfway through 2020, as the publication of my debut novel, *The Fear*, approached, I wanted to offer a free quick read for my newsletter subscribers. I knew I wanted something pulpy, something that hooks you from the start. At the time I was finding a new appreciation for the horror subgenre of slashers. Binging the *Friday the 13th* franchise and reading slasher fiction from authors like Stephen Graham Jones and Adam Cesare. So when I stumbled on that fateful image of a smiley face with its skull ripping through in burst seams of blood, the fully formed idea—of an abandoned amusement park whose mascot still lives on—was born. I knew without a shadow of a doubt that this was a story that wanted to grow past the constraints of one free novella. Though, I will admit, I had no idea just how much it wanted to grow. Even now, I feel it pushing against the boundaries I've built it, growling that it wants more, that it's *hungry*. I'll probably let it expand wherever it wishes. I'm not sure I could stop it if I wanted to.

Before I wrote *Welcome to Smileyland*, however, I was in talks with the publisher Blood Rites Horror about a possible graphic novel. We decided to test out the waters with a three-page comic in their second issue of the fiction, poetry, and art magazine *SPINE*. I spat out a quick script and Jay Alexander (then using the *nom de plume* of Nick Harper—#NickHarperLives!) similarly spat out a quick illustration and lettering. You may still be able to find this issue of *SPINE*, entitled "All Hallow's Eve," floating around the Internet, but don't take my word on that.

Once I'd written the first full adventure into this world, my 1990s queer slasher novella *Welcome to Smiley-land*, I realized that many of the details established in our three-page comic (which we entitled "Smile, It's Halloween!") had changed. This is a normal and necessary part of the writing process, but it still bugged me.

Enter *Sister Funtime*. Because it technically took place before the amusement park had even been built, I knew my newest novella needed a framing device that anchored it in Mister Smiley's world. And just like that, I saw an opportunity to retcon the early errors of "Smile, It's Halloween!"

Those of you who have read the comic may recognize the dialogue from the first three and a half pages of this book. I copied them down word for word, warts and all, as a way to preserve the comic for the sake of posterity.

But then, instead of recreating that final image, I let Jess step forward and correct Brad's mistakes one by one. Then—bless Jess for this—she turned to the story at hand, of an innocent nun slowly descending into madness.

Smileyland has many beginnings—and I mean that in two different ways. Its worldbuilding origins have been many and varied: at first I thought the origin story was of a young boy who is abandoned at Smileyland only to grow into a serial killer; then, I thought it was blueprints in the basement of an orphanage about to burn down; now, I believe its origins can be traced hundreds of years even before *that*! But also, it has a few different publishing beginnings as well: first, that "Smile, It's Halloween!" comic in *SPINE*; then, the *Welcome to Smileyland* novella as a free ebook download from my website (it's still there, go grab a copy!); and now, in what may be argued as the *official* beginnings, with this published novella in your hands, *Sister Funtime*.

Now that you know where it all began, you're probably wondering where we go from here. Well, I think I know exactly where I'd like to take you, what's coming next and what it's all leading to. But I'm not telling. Not yet.

What is that strange breathing creature deep underground?

Why did Mary's crucifix cut it off from the world with that cave-in?

Who exactly is Mr. James, and where is he now?

And were those blueprints lost with the orphanage? Or will Smileyland find a way?

All the answers to these questions are forthcoming. For now, I hope you've enjoyed the journey so far. As you wait for more, be sure to come on inside, smile wide, and don't forget to say your prayers.

Welcome . . . to Smileyland.

Spencer Hamilton
December 2021

WANT MORE SMILEYLAND?

Welcome, welcome, welcome to Smileyland! High schoolers Ramirez and friends go on a late-night adventure into a long-abandoned amusement park in upstate New York. When the bodies start to pile up, Ramirez must discover who is behind the Mister Smiley mask before it's too late.

Grab this free slasher novella by joining my newsletter now!

Make sure you don't miss any Smileyland news by staying up-to-date with my newsletter from www.SpencerHamiltonBooks.com!

I've got big plans for Smileyland and Sister Funtime and Mister Smiley . . .

ABOUT THE AUTHOR

Spencer Hamilton is an LGBTQIA+ author of horror. His debut collection, *Kitchen Sink*, and debut novel, *The Fear*, were published in 2020. His work has appeared in several anthologies, the most recent being Blood Rites Horror's *Bitter Chills: Holiday Edition* and the upcoming *Dead of Night*. He is co-editor of the forthcoming queer horror anthology *Camp Horror*. He lives in Philadelphia with his family.

You can find him at www.SpencerHamiltonBooks.com or on Instagram (@nerdywordsmith) or Twitter (@SHamiltonBooks), where he is occasionally clever.